Abby's Fabulous Season

Abby's Fabulous Season

Alain M. Bergeron

Translation by Chantal Bilodeau

Second Story Press

Library and Archives Canada Cataloguing in Publication

Bergeron, Alain M., 1957-
[Fabuleuse saison d'Abby Hoffman. English]
Abby's fabulous season / by Alain M. Bergeron ; translated by Chantal Bilodeau.

Translation of: La fabuleuse saison d'Abby Hoffman.
Issued in print and electronic formats.
ISBN 978-1-927583-47-0 (pbk.).—ISBN 978-1-927583-48-7 (epub)

1. Hoffman, Abby—Juvenile fiction. I. Bilodeau, Chantal, 1968-,
translator. II. Title. III. Title: Fabuleuse saison d'Abby Hoffman. English.

PS8553.E67454F3113 2014   jC843'.54   C2014-903673-6

C2014-903674-4

Translation by Chantal Bilodeau
Edited by Carolyn Jackson
Designed by Melissa Kaita
Cover art © Carl Pelletier (Polygone Studio)

Printed and bound in Canada

Acknowledgement
The author would like to thank the Canada Council for the Arts for awarding him a grant in
support of the research and writing of this novel.

Second Story Press gratefully acknowledges the support of the Ontario Arts Council and
the Canada Council for the Arts for our publishing program. We acknowledge the financial
support of the Government of Canada through the Canada Book Fund.

For its support of this translation, we thank the Canada Council for the Arts. We acknowledge
the financial support of the Government of Canada through the National Translation Program
for Book Publishing, an initiative of the *Roadmap for Canada's Official Languages 2013-2018:
Education, Immigration, Communities*, for our translation activities.

ONTARIO ARTS COUNCIL
CONSEIL DES ARTS DE L'ONTARIO
50 YEARS OF ONTARIO GOVERNMENT SUPPORT OF THE ARTS
50 ANS DE SOUTIEN DU GOUVERNEMENT DE L'ONTARIO AUX ARTS

Canada Council   Conseil des Arts
for the Arts   du Canada

MIX
Paper from
responsible sources
FSC
www.fsc.org   FSC® C004071

Published by
Second Story Press
20 Maud Street, Suite 401
Toronto, ON M5V 2M5
www.secondstorypress.ca

To the one and only Abby Hoffman,
to her brothers Paul, Muni, and Benny,
and to the memory of their parents,
Dorothy Medhurst and Samuel H. Hoffman.

*"Only she who attempts the absurd will achieve
the impossible..."*
(These words appear on a plaque in homage to
Abby Hoffman at the University of Toronto's
Hart House – 1979)

Hockey Then and Now

At the time that Abby Hoffman played a season in the Little Toronto Hockey League, the game was quite different. Players in the 1950s didn't wear helmets or face shields or face cages, and being a good hockey player almost automatically meant being aggressive on the ice. Even body checking was legal then, and often encouraged. Today's young players are not allowed to body check the way the players in Abby's league did, so don't try it! And now helmets, face guards, and goalie masks are mandatory, making the game safer for today's players. But there's one thing that hasn't changed—kids still love to play hockey!

Little Toronto Hockey League Resumes November 19 at Varsity

The Toronto Hockey League will again foster the Little Toronto Hockey League series at Varsity. Purpose of this league is to teach boys how to play hockey. The series is open to boys 9, 10 and 11 years of age as of August 1, 1955, living in the Metropolitan area, who are not playing or members of any organized hockey team other than their own school.

Registration for participation in the Little Toronto Hockey League will take place on Saturday, November 19, from 5 until 7 p.m. at Varsity Arena (Bloor at Bedford Rd.). Boys are asked to bring skates, hockey stick and birth certificate. They will be allowed to skate until 7:15 p.m. after being registered.

Admission fee is 25 cents per night and will remain the same all season. For any further information, please get in touch with the chairman of the league, Earl Graham.

(from *Toronto Daily Star*, Saturday November 12, 1955; page 24)

FIRST PERIOD
November 19, 1955 to February 27, 1956

Chapter 1

As soon as I step into the room filled with young people, most of them with their parents, I can see I'm already the exception.

Only boys! Hundreds of them! All here for the information session about the Little Toronto Hockey League's upcoming season. Boys of all ages—from young kids holding their parents' hands to teenagers who have come alone on this cold November evening of 1955.

My mother—slim in her long, beige winter coat—spots three empty chairs toward the back. With her chin, she indicates two more chairs in the center of the room for my big brothers, Paul and Muni. They rush to take the seats, happy they won't be seen with their mother, a two-year-old toddler and, worst of all, their little sister.

I sit at the back between my parents and take off my coat. The crowd is enough to warm up the place. I can't imagine what a summer meeting like this, in the middle of June for baseball registration, would be like. Phew! I would die from the heat.

But tonight, for reasons of my own, I pull my hat all the way down to my ears, and keep my hair tucked inside.

No matter how hard I look, I can't find a single girl. Yes! There's my best friend Susie Read, a few rows in front of us. But she's not here for hockey. She's here with her younger brother. Susie's sport is figure skating—which is closer to ballet than to a real sport, if you ask me.

I've tried it—figure skating, not ballet—and I hated it right off the bat! A skating rink is not supposed to be for dancing. It's for skating, stick in hand, while chasing a frozen rubber puck at crazy speed and jostling boys. Now we're talking!

Next to us a man lights a cigarette, takes a big puff, and blows the smoke toward the ceiling. My father—like my mother—believes in sports because of the health benefits. He gives the man a disapproving look and says, "You think smoking like a chimney in a closed room is good for children?" My youngest brother, Little Benny, is sitting on his lap.

The man, cigarette hanging from his lips, blows a

cloud of smoke in my father's face. What a creep!

"Hah! As long as the meeting doesn't last too long....
A little smoke has never hurt anyone. If your baby has an
ear infection, I can cure it by blowing in his ear."

I can tell my father is fighting the urge to rip the
cigarette from the man's mouth and crush it under his
heel. Or better yet, put it out on the guy's forehead.

Lots of the adults here tonight smoke. My parents don't. But right now they're second-hand smoking,
just like Benny and me. A cloud hangs above us and
partly hides the overhead banner that reads: SPORT IS
HEALTH! *Not in this room!*

The crowd is growing impatient. The meeting should
have started fifteen minutes ago. Those are precious minutes subtracted from the skating session that is to follow
the registration—the reason so many boys, and one girl,
have brought sticks and skates.

Now there's some movement up front—a man
climbing onto the podium and walking toward the
microphone. It's enough to create silence.

Earl Graham, whose shiny, bald head makes him
look older than my father, introduces himself. He's the
chairman of the Little Toronto Hockey League. He's not
very tall and rather pudgy, and he seems a bit nervous.
His huge glasses rest on chubby cheeks.

"Good evening, Ladies and Gentlemen, and hello
boys!" he exclaims in a cheerful voice.

Boys…. Quite a beginning!

After a boring introduction, Mr. Graham explains, mostly for the parents' benefit, the general rules of the 1955-56 season.

"The most important thing is not to win, but to play. The youngest players, regardless of their abilities, will spend the same amount of time on the ice as their team-mates," assures the chairman.

After tonight's registration, the players will be categorized by age, then divided into teams. The boys—*it's an obsession!*—will be informed by phone about their team's first game. There will be a dozen games in the season, including the playoffs.

"Those of you who were with us in previous years know all of this already. However, we have something new this year," he continues. "Toward the end of the season, we'll gather the best players in each age category into an all-star team. The team will then compete in an inter-league game here in Toronto."

This news is received with wild applause. Some parents can already see their sons on the team, even though they haven't stepped onto the ice yet.

"Questions?" asks Mr. Graham.

As he seems to expect, several hands shoot up. A lady with a funny hat that looks like an ashtray shares her concerns. "Last year, my son didn't like his coach. How do you intend to address similar situations this year?"

Embarrassed by his mother's question, the son, sitting next to her, buries his face in his coat.

A man standing two rows behind her pipes up. "Last year, my son didn't play enough. It decreased his chances of being recruited in the National League. What assurance do I have that he'll play regularly this year?"

And another...

"My son has to be in the same team as his best friend!" says an adult with an impressive white beard worthy of a fake Santa Claus.

There are no general questions, or very few; only individual cases calling for individual answers. Mr. Graham patiently invites these people to come and talk to him afterwards.

Actually, one of the rare good questions is asked by—my father.

"Are there girls' teams this season, Mr. Graham?"

Finally, an interesting subject! About time. I'm squirming with excitement. But my enthusiasm is short-lived.

"No. For now, nothing justifies the creation of a league for little girls," he answers in a flat voice.

Little girls…. Ugh!

"Girls can't play hockey anyway," says a boy in front of me. Other boys—all idiots—approve noisily. My mother puts a hand on my shoulder to stop me from getting up and replying to that stupid comment. If this boy was my opponent on the ice, I'd show him!

Mr. Graham informs us that the registration for figure skating will be next week.

I'm in shock. Does this mean I won't be able to play hockey? Because I'm certainly capable of it! I throw a fierce glance at my parents while Mr. Graham announces that registration for the kids' hockey season is now open.

All of a sudden, there's chaos. The organizers do their best to maintain some kind of order, but they're clearly overwhelmed as everyone rushes to sign up.

My mother follows my two big brothers to register them in a higher age category. I envy them! It's so unfair. I feel like crying. I put my coat on, ready to leave.

My father puts his arm around my shoulders. It barely comforts me.

"You know, Abby," he says with a mischievous smile, "I didn't hear anything tonight that forbids girls from playing hockey." He stands up, lifting Little Benny onto his shoulders. "Come with me."

My father pulls me toward the registration table for my age group, the eight-to-ten year-olds. Several parents are clustered around the table, anxious to get this over with. The two people facing the impatient mob—a man and a woman with gray hair—manage the crowd as best they can.

The organizers regularly remind people to stay calm. As soon as a volunteer completes a registration, the next parents rudely shove their son's birth certificate under his nose.

My parents have always encouraged us to be proactive. A new registration table is being set up to try to deal with the crowd. Without telling my father, who is talking to another parent, I head to the new table and suddenly find myself first in line. Doubt creeps in. *What if they turn me away? What if…*It's getting hotter and hotter in here. I'm sweating in my winter coat and my hat.

"Go ahead," says a man with a pen in his hand. "We don't have all night." I show him my birth certificate, but without giving it to him. My thumb hides the letter F— for Female.

"Abigail Golda Hoffman? That's a funny name for a boy," he remarks.

I give him a half-smile. "It's true. I don't know any boy named Golda," I say.

"There aren't enough boxes for all the letters in your name," he observes. "How about we settle for Ab Hoffman—is that okay with you?"

He writes my name in abbreviated form along with my age, address, and phone number. "What position do you play, son?" the man asks me.

Son? Normally I would be insulted. But not now. If I must be transformed into a boy to play hockey, then so be it.

"Defense…I'm a defenseMAN," I say nervously.

I sign at the bottom of the form. He keeps the original and gives me a copy.

"Thank you very much," I say. "And good luck with the rest of the evening." I fold the form and put it in my coat pocket. I can't see my father anywhere, so I decide to get on the ice of Varsity Arena while I still have a little time.

Dozens of boys are already handling the puck and outsmarting invisible opponents. This is no different than the games at the outdoor rink in front of my house. And I'm solid on my skates; I don't turn over on my ankles like the boys who hold onto the boards. I can easily keep up with those who have the wind in their hair. I hit the puck as hard as most. I feel great!

Suddenly, I see my parents and my two big brothers near the boards. I approach, a grin of satisfaction on my face.

"Hey! It's done!" I say.

"What?" asks Paul. "You're going to play hockey?"

"With boys?" adds Muni.

I show them the registration form.

"Who's Ab Hoffman?" asks Paul. "I didn't know you had another brother at home."

"Yeah, he even has the same birthday as you!" notes Muni.

My father fakes surprise when he looks at the form. "They must have made a mistake…"

"We don't have to correct it, right, Dad?" I ask.

My father is amused. "Only if you insist."

On the drive home I sit between my two big brothers, trying to ignore their sarcastic remarks about the place of girls on an ice rink.

"Girls do figure skating," declares Paul.

"Yeah! They don't play hockey," adds Muni.

"Guys!" says Dad.

Ab Hoffman…Yes, I can live with that!

Chapter 2

I'm so excited at the idea of playing in the Little Toronto Hockey League that I can't fall asleep. I twist and turn for about an hour until I'm so exasperated that I get up. I try to keep the noise down so I don't wake up Little Benny or my parents who are snoring in the next room. There's only one way to relax at such a late hour.

As quiet as a mouse, I get dressed, put on my coat and slip out of the house.

The cold November air is invigorating. No trace of snow yet, but the ground has been frozen since Halloween. The late autumn has been marked by cold weather. To my brothers' great relief, the lawn mower was confined to the garage as soon as the grass stopped growing and turned to dull yellow.

Although every season has its charm in Canada, the winter is by far my favorite, because of hockey.

With my skates slung over my shoulder and my hockey stick in my hand, I cross the street and head for the neighborhood rink outside of Humberside Collegiate. My brothers and I are lucky to live just a few steps away. Given how cold it's been over the last several days, the people in charge have decided to open the rink two weeks early. For me, Christmas arrived in mid-November this year. Every time I have a few minutes, I put on my skates and come here.

I started skating at this rink when I was three and a half years old. That's already way in the past, but I remember the first time I showed up with a hockey stick—I was just past five. I had such a good time. Unlike many kids my age, boys included, I used the stick to hit the puck, not to prop myself up!

Even though my brothers are sometimes—not often, but sometimes—real pains, they showed me how. I wasn't allowed to play with the older kids because it was too dangerous. But I enjoyed handling the puck and skating without losing it. I would shoot against the boards and the sound of the puck hitting the wood made the most beautiful sound: *THOCK!*

Since last year, I've been allowed to play with the

older kids. All guys. Girls are happy to do figure skating in the other half of the huge rink, which is divided in two by a large gate. My friend, Susie Read, is a champion figure skater. She comes to the rink too, and does figures. She jumps off one foot and lands on the other. She spins around without ever losing her balance.

Without my stick, I feel naked. And what about those teeth they put in the front of "girl" skates? As for skating style, girls don't glide to go forward, they push.

Spinning around by myself with my arms stuck out doesn't interest me. Being graceful and delicate, wearing a pretty dress and a fancy hat, and probably even perfume and make-up? No, thank you!

I would rather skate at top speed, brake and stop on a dime, take off in the opposite direction to protect my goalie, and knock an opponent against the boards—that's what I love! After the *THOCK!*, the *Hnghk!* the player makes when I crush him is music to my ear.

Tonight there will be no *Hnghk!* because I'm alone at the moonlit rink. It's magical. I should be sound asleep, but instead, I'm dreaming with my eyes wide open! This whole space is just for me.

I hurry to put on my skates. My fingers are cold. I should have put on my skates in the warm house, as usual. But I was afraid the noise might wake up someone and put an end to my plans. So I can suffer a little—nothing will beat the joy I'm about to feel.

There! My coat is off. I'm wearing my Canadiens jersey, the one my brothers wore before me. Now I'm ready…

The game is on, Abby Hoffman!

The night is so still that every time I hit the puck the sound seems amplified tenfold. I don't dare shoot the puck against the boards. The noise might wake up the entire neighborhood.

I just love the sound of the blade digging into the ice to propel me forward…

In my head, I'm no longer alone—two teams are facing each other. I'm defending the colors of the Detroit Red Wings against the Montreal Canadiens. My coach, Jimmy Skinner, sends me into the game with less than a minute to play. The score is tied 4-4.

"The outcome is in your gloves, my boy!"

My boy! That's a good one!

After the faceoff, the puck flies into my zone. I grab it. Positioned behind the net, I watch my teammates spread in front of me. No one is able to break free from his opponent.

"Quick, Ab! Time's running out!" shouts Coach Skinner.

I have no choice. I charge ahead and come out of my protective bubble. Immediately, an opponent rushes toward me. With a skillful deke I slide the puck between his skates. A second opponent shows up. I try to pass the puck to a teammate, but he falls down. I turn my head to the left and trick my opponent.

I cross the red line. Huh! I didn't know someone had painted zone lines on the ice of the Humberside rink....

I skate at full speed and easily overtake two opponents. Where are my teammates? They're watching me and encouraging me to keep going.

"All the way to the end, Ab!"

The coach uses both hands to indicate there are only ten seconds left. I skate around the defenseman while protecting the puck.

"...5!...4!...3!..." count thousands of spectators sitting in the bleachers.

Once I reach the goalie, I let loose a backhand. The puck bounces off the crossbar and falls behind the goal line. The red light comes on a second before the end of the game.

We won! We won!

The announcer's voice explodes through the microphone while my teammates and a crowd of fans who have invaded the rink surround me and congratulate me.

"The winning goal of the Detroit Red Wings was scored by Ab Hoffman!"

The standing ovation that follows gives me goose bumps. Among the fans, I see my parents waving at me. My mother approaches. Instead of congratulating me, she gently takes me by the shoulders.

"Abby! Abby! Girl…"

"Shhh! Mom, it's a secret. They don't know…"

My mother lightly shakes me. "Abby! Abby. You're late for school. Wake up! Time to get out of bed!"

Wh…what? School?

Oh, no!

Chapter 3

I feel like someone who has pulled off a good prank. It must show on my face because Susie brings it up in the schoolyard during recess.

"Abby, you have that mischievous smile again, like your father. What are you hiding?" she whispers before jumping rope and singing: "Ice cream soda, lemonade, punch. Spell the initials of your honey bunch. A-B-C-D…"

I'm holding one end of the rope and turning without much enthusiasm. I would rather play dodge ball with the boys. Susie is all smiles. She's spinning around, an obvious reminder of her talent as a figure skater.

I can't spin around like that. But I can skate forward, turn on a dime, and go backwards. I know for a lot of boys my age, that's nearly impossible. I see them at my neighborhood rink—instead of skating backwards, they go sideways. They think they can hide their lack of skill that way. For someone playing defense, it's ridiculous.

Susie trips on the rope at the letter R—for Ronald, her class neighbor. I think she does it on purpose because it's not the first time she has stopped jumping at the letter R. She's a jump rope expert so she stops exactly where and when she wants. She's clever, that Susie! She'd love it if Ronnie were her ice-cream-soda-lemonade honey bunch. But no chance of that today. After a girl tells him that Susie called his name, Ronald flees to the other side of the schoolyard.

For me, boys are only interesting when they have skates on their feet, a stick in their hands, and they're chasing a puck.

Susie abandons the jump rope and drags me over to play hopscotch. "So?" she says, while hopping happily toward the word HEAVEN.

"So what?"

Susie stops on the numbers 7 and 8 and, looking indignant, puts her hands on her hips. "You're keeping secrets from me!" she scolds.

I shrug. Why not tell her after all? "I'm going to play hockey, Susie—"

She makes a face, irritated. "That's not a secret. You already play hockey, Abby Hoffman!"

"You don't understand, Susie Read!" I say, lowering my voice to make sure no one else hears me. "I'm going to play hockey with boys in—"

"I know!" she interrupts, annoyed.

"With boys...in the Little Toronto Hockey League."

"*WHAT?*" she exclaims.

So much for being discreet. If there were snow on the ground, I'd rub her face in it to shut her up. That would teach her!

Seeing my angry expression, Susie apologizes. She's embarrassed by her outburst. "You...you registered? How did you do that?"

I tell her the story of the previous evening.

"Ab Hoffman?" she repeats, incredulous. "Is that a boy's name?"

"Well, more so than Abby or Abigail."

She looks around to make sure no one is eavesdropping. "Boys are not idiots, or at least some of them aren't. They'll figure out that you're not one of them pretty fast."

I have my argument ready. "My mother promised to cut my hair very short tonight."

"You think they'll fall for it? It's obvious that you're a girl."

"Yes, but that's because you know me, Susie. I'll be in a league where no one knows who I am."

"Or what you are," she adds. "A girl who plays hockey in a boys' league!" My friend covers her mouth. She blushes as if she's just had a shameful thought. I can guess what it is.

"The players in our age group don't get dressed in the locker room—they get dressed at home. That's how it was for my brothers. I'll only have my skates and my jersey to put on. As for showering after the game, most players take showers at home."

For reasons of her own, Susie seems disappointed. She tries again.

"Yes, but what happens if a boy does decide to take a shower?"

Are showers an obsession with her? I smile. "Well…I'll bury my face in my hands, like this." I can see Susie's face through my fingers. She scolds me again and laughs.

"You're looking through your fingers, you bad girl! Hey, do you need help taking off your skates after the game?"

"I have a better idea. Why don't you give up figure skating and play hockey with me?"

My friend turns her back to me. "Out of the question! It's a sport for bullies!"

⬤

"Guys," warns Mom, "stop teasing your sister!"

When it comes to annoying me, Paul and Muni

usually show no restraint. We're in the kitchen. My mother is cutting my hair, as promised. And my brothers are circling me like vultures ready to swoop down on their prey. But this time, they're outdoing themselves!

My mother trims the hair around my ears and on my forehead.

"Aren't you afraid of being bodychecked by an opponent?" says Paul.

"It won't be the time to cry and ask for your mommy," adds Muni, making a face.

"It's those guys who'll cry for their mommies after I knock them against the boards!"

My brothers snicker. My father, who is changing Little Benny's diaper, orders his sons to finish doing the dishes.

"Girls who play hockey…" Muni begins.

"…and guys who do the dishes. The world is upside down," concludes Paul.

"Welcome to the twentieth century," says Dad.

My mother doesn't usually fear for her only daughter. I'm no fragile doll. But her expression tells me that she's worried. "If a boy wants to fight with you, Abby, what will you do?"

Without hesitating, I raise a fist. "After this, he'll run home crying!"

Paul jumps in. "If you want, we'll teach you, Ab."

My mother corrects him right away. "In this house, it's Abby! Don't you forget it, you two."

Muni steps forward, his right hand closed into a fist. "You hit between the eyes, Ab…"

My mother interrupts the hair cutting and glares at him.

"…ee," he finishes. "Ab-ee!"

With a nod of the head, my mother sends him back to his brother, and to their pots and pans.

"The players are forbidden to fight, Abby," Dad remarks, more for Mom's benefit than for mine.

My mother presses my head forward so she can shave my neck. She's very skilled. I hear my brothers whisper. What evil plan are they concocting?

Even though she's absorbed in her task, my mother calls them to order. "Finish the dishes before you go outside to play hockey."

"We'll be right back, Mom," promises Paul.

My head is down but I can guess from the sound of their footsteps that they're going to their bedroom. The noises that follow tell me they're looking for something. What they're in such a hurry to find, I don't know.

"I have it!" shouts Muni.

"Me too!" says Paul.

They come running back to the kitchen. My mother lifts up my head—the haircut is finished. My brothers are impressed.

"For a girl, you look like a boy!" says Paul, surprised.

"No. You look like Curious Georgette!" says Muni with a burst of laughter shared by our older brother. He means my favorite comic book character, the monkey *Curious George*.

My father is still busy with the diaper changing. He wrinkles his nose at the smell. "Well!" exclaims Dad, after taking a look at me. "Dorothy, we now have three boys who play hockey!"

"But one who plays like a girl!" adds Paul.

My mother hands me a mirror. My hair has never been this short.

"Thank you, Mom! I'm sure it's going to work." I will easily blend into the crowd of male players.

"You're only missing one thing," observes Paul.

"Yeah," Muni continues. "Any boy who plays hockey must have one…otherwise…"

"One what?" I ask.

A few inches from my nose, they dangle…a jock!

"It's to protect your privates during the games," says Paul, trying to hide a smile.

"It's part of the normal equipment for a boy who plays hockey. If you don't wear a jock, you can't call yourself a boy," insists Muni.

"Guys!" says Mom, pretending to be offended.

My father, who has finished changing Benny's diaper, steps in. "Your brothers are right, Abby. It's an item that…uh…shows, even under hockey pants."

Happy and surprised to get their father's support, my brothers let loose. "You have to understand, Abby," begins Paul. "If the puck hits it, we have to hear the sound."

"The sound? What sound?"

My parents are amused by the turn of the conversation.

Muni answers: "The sound…*POCK!* Not as in a hockey puck. *POCK!* Like when the puck hits the jock."

"Yes, you need a *POCK!*" says Paul, hitting the jock with his knuckles. *POCK! POCK! POCK!*

"Because if there's no *POCK!*" continues Muni, "it won't be believable. No *POCK!* It's SCHLOCK! like the boys say."

"The boys say that?" asks Mom.

"I believe it," interjects Dad. "The jock is as important a piece of equipment as shoulder pads or leg pads."

"It's true, I almost forgot," says Mom, with a touch of irony. "It's essential protection! Yet no helmet for the head. It's not hard to figure out where male priorities are."

"It doesn't take much to get injured, Mom," remarks Paul.

"No, it doesn't take much," she repeats, turning up her nose at her sons' jocks.

Then she addresses me. "Abby, make sure you don't neglect to wear this highly specialized piece of equipment."

I get up from my chair and ruffle my hair. "Okay, Mom."

POCK! POCK! POCK! my brothers keep repeating in my ear.

The ringing of the phone drowns out the *POCK*s. Paul shoves Muni aside. At the Hoffmans, there are two subjects of discord: whether the Canadiens, Maple Leafs, or Red Wings have the best team, and who will answer the phone.

However, as soon as someone puts a hand on the receiver, the fight is over. Just like when a referee calls an offside and the players stop skating.

"Hello?" says Paul.

"Uh? There's no Ab here. You have the wrong number." He hangs up. "It was for someone named Ab!"

It's a good thing my father held me back, otherwise I would have shoved my stupid brother's jock down his throat.

"That was for me! For my hockey registration!" I say, my voice breaking.

My mother points a threatening finger at Paul—not a good sign at all. "You. I don't want you touching the phone for the rest of the week, is that clear?"

Muni applauds the punishment imposed on his older brother. "It's simple: A plus B equals AB! Like our sister Abby!"

"If he doesn't call back, I will have missed my only

chance to play hockey in a real league," I say with tears in my eyes.

My brother lowers his head. "I'm sorry."

The ringing of the phone resonates throughout the house again. Muni is about to pick up but my father slaps his fingers.

"Ow!" he moans, quickly withdrawing his hand.

"Hands off!" orders Dad. "Your voice sounds almost the same as Paul's. The person might think he's dialled the wrong number again. Abby will get it."

"It's not fair!" complains Muni.

"Oh yes, it is!" gloats Paul.

I pick up. "Hello?" I immediately regret opening my mouth. I'm nervous, so my voice is high-pitched and clear—like a girl's. "Yes, this is Ab Hoffman...ahem... ahem..." I try to make my voice deeper.

The man, whose name is Al Grossi, if I understood correctly, is the coach of the St. Catharines Tee Pees. He tells me that I'm part of his team, and that the first game will be Saturday at 8:00 a.m. at Varsity Arena.

"Will I be there? Of course, I'll be there!"

I try to contain my excitement but under the circumstances, it's very difficult. My dream to play hockey in a league is becoming reality.

"My position? Defense...left...okay.... I'll be number 6? Oh—"

My father gives me the thumbs up: That's Floyd

Curry's number, his favorite Canadiens player. No Red Wings player wears that number.

My mother comes out of the bedroom with my brothers trailing behind her. Their ears are red! I raise a fist to the ceiling as a sign of victory. My mother applauds silently, without her hands touching, and gives me a huge grin. Even Paul and Muni are happy for me.

Mr. Grossi also explains that, as I expected, we have to put on our equipment at home. Except for the skates, which we can put on in the locker room. The jerseys will be given to the players at the first game.

"Don't forget to say thank you," whispers Dad.

"Thank you," I repeat like a robot. "See you on Saturday." I hang up.

It's as if a huge weight has been lifted from my shoulders. I suddenly feel as light as a feather. I'm so happy I could almost kiss my brothers. *Ew, no*—I can live without that.

I grab a pen and note Saturday's game on our activity board. The bulletin board on the other wall is used to pin newspaper clippings that capture the attention of the Hoffman family.

I write on the Toronto Maple Leafs calendar: Ab...8:00 a.m., Varsity Arena. On the photo, forward George Armstrong seems to be looking me in the eye and smiling from the corner of his mouth as if to say: "Well done, Ab!"

"The Tee Pees?" repeats Paul. "Do you know, Abby, that the name of your team comes from the initials of the company Thompson Products?"

"I thought you were only interested in rocks, Paul," remarks Muni.

"It was a research project in one of my classes last year," my older brother explains.

I rush to my room to put on my pajamas and read a *Curious George* story before going to bed. Following his adventures relaxes me.

"In bed so early?" says Mom, surprised. "It's only 7:30."

"I want to be in shape for the game."

"It's in three days," Dad reminds me. "Today is Wednesday."

Still all this time to wait. It'll be unbearable....

Chapter 4

At school, my short hair is a big hit. Some students confuse me for a boy, which is very good news.

"Aren't you insulted, Abby?" worries Susie Read.

"No! This is exactly what I want to hear!"

When Ms. Morley asks about my new haircut, I stress the practical aspect. "It dries faster after swimming classes." My answer seems to satisfy the teacher and my classmates. The subject is quickly forgotten.

Ms. Morley draws our attention to a strange drawing on the blackboard done by a student—Eve Lismer. It shows someone with a big head and a messy scrawl in the middle of it.

"That," says Eve, indicating the scribble "is the brain.

It helps us to think. When you don't have one, like boys, you can't tell the difference between a salamander and a chameleon."

Saturday seems so far away. I've never found it so hard to wait for a special day—and I include Christmas along with my birthday, February 11th. But there's no better way to kill time when you're waiting for a hockey game than to play hockey! My parents are understanding and respect their kids' interests. Once our homework is done, they allow us to go to the ice rink across the street, before and after dinner.

During the meal, my brothers shower me with conflicting advice.

"When a player charges at you, don't pay attention to the puck," declares Paul.

"What are you talking about?" interjects Muni. "Forget about the player! You have to pay attention to the puck!"

My father suggests a compromise—deal with the player first, and then with the puck.

"That's what I said, Dad!" exclaim both my brothers together.

The night before my first game, I'm so excited I can't sleep. The *tic-toc* of the alarm clock drives me crazy. The fact that I can't get comfortable doesn't help either; to save precious minutes, I didn't put on my pajamas. I wore my hockey stuff instead—all of it except the skates.

Every few minutes, I make sure that my alarm clock is set for 6:00 a.m. The last thing I need is to be late.

My nightmare comes true a few hours later when Paul and Muni rush into my room.

"Get up, Abby!" shouts Paul.

"You're late!" Muni yells, looking at his watch in horror.

Oh, no! And I'm not dreaming. This is real life. Ow! I just pinched my arm to be sure. I leap out of bed and rush to the kitchen. It's still dark. Very dark! I switch on the light.

Something's not right. My brothers have the kind of mischievous smiles that spell trouble. Meanwhile, I'm having a hard time getting organized. Food? Yes! I grab a banana from the fruit bowl and pour myself a glass of orange juice.

Paul fills a glass with water. Then he pours the glass into another glass. He keeps going back and forth like that for several seconds. The running water suddenly changes the order of my priorities. Never mind the juice. I have to go to the bathroom, and fast!

Really, going to bed wearing my hockey equipment wasn't one of my brightest ideas. And why does the urge to pee become ten times worse as soon as I see the toilet?

I have to hurry. But the problem is that I have several pieces of equipment to take off. Including a jock!

Phew! I made it…but it was close!

I hear steps coming from my parents' bedroom. All of a sudden, my brain starts working. How come they're not awake yet? My mother is always the first one up in the morning. Is she late too? Didn't her alarm go off? Normally, she would have had my breakfast ready way before I opened my eyes.

I flush, wash my hands, and put my equipment back on. Then I hear a door slam shut. My brothers' bedroom door. Apparently, they've fled from the kitchen.

And then it dawns on me. Oh! Those morons!

My mother, wrapped in her bathrobe, gives me a strange look. "What are you doing up in the middle of the night?"

Just as I'm about to explain, she notices my clothes and bursts out laughing. "Abby, you didn't sleep like that, did you?"

"Well, I didn't really sleep," I say, sighing. I'm annoyed. My brothers fooled me. They're the ones who suggested I wear my hockey equipment as pajamas. And they're the ones who woke me up in the middle of the night.

My mother glances at the kitchen clock. It's 3:45.

"We'll talk about this over breakfast. Go back to bed, Abby. And for heaven's sake, put on your pajamas!"

"I'm afraid I'll be late," I tell her as she leads me back to my room.

She kisses me on the cheek. "Good night. Hop into bed now. I have to go say a few words to your brothers."

I smile under the covers when I hear voices in my brothers' room.

"Mom, do you really think we would get up in the middle of the night to play a prank on our beloved sister?" says Paul.

"Mom, it's impossible. We were sleeping! Abby must have had a nightmare," adds Muni.

I fall asleep imagining them skating around the rink in front of thousands of spectators, wearing only their jocks...

Hysterical!

—

At six o'clock, the sound of alarm clocks echoes through the entire house. My parents' alarm is the first one to go silent, then mine. Huh, strange...my brothers' alarm is still blaring. Mom turns it off.

This is unusual for the weekend. Normally, the boys don't stir until almost noon. Did Mom make my brothers set their alarm this early? Maybe she was punishing them for waking me up in the middle of the night. In a drowsy voice, Paul says he didn't want me to be late this morning. That's possible. Paul and Muni are capable of the worst... and also the best. At any rate, I'm not mad at them. It was fair game. But they better watch out.

So now the whole family is up and gathered around the table to devour the breakfast that my father put together. The conversation turns to the National Hockey League's results from the previous day.

Dad and Paul believe that the Montreal Canadiens are the team to watch this year. According to them, Montreal—with Jean Béliveau, Maurice Richard, and goalie Jacques Plante—can win it all. A little like my mother, Muni can't think beyond the Toronto Maple Leafs. As for me? I think the Detroit Red Wings—the last Stanley Cup Champions—have a good chance.

I don't have a favorite player. My father loves Floyd Curry of the Canadiens. As a right winger, he's not the most flamboyant scorer—actually, far from it—but he excels on defense. I'll try to make myself into a Floyd Curry today and honor his number 6.

"Should we get ready?" suggests Dad. "We have to leave the house at 7:30 at the latest. By the time we drive to the arena and Abby puts on her skates, we won't be too early."

As we get up from the table, my mother warns Paul and Muni. "Don't forget, boys. As soon as we pass this door, it's Ab and not Abby."

My brothers nod. "Yes! Yes! We know!"

"Abby! Abby!" repeats Little Benny.

I rush to my room to put on my equipment. I keep my jeans on and slip the hockey pants over them, as well as the stockings, which have holes in the knees, and the leg and shoulder pads. It only takes me a few minutes to get ready. I can't wait!

Muni joins me, with Paul in tow. "Did you remember everything?" he asks.

He doesn't have to explain what everything means…

POCK! POCK!

"Yes," I grin. *Everything* is in place.

Paul brings my hockey stick from the hall closet. He hands it to me in a solemn way.

"Don't you notice anything?"

I examine the stick. Is he pulling another prank on me? "Did you saw it so it'll break when I shoot?"

Paul claims innocence. "Who do you think I am? Muni?"

"Hey!" says Muni, offended. "I changed the tape around the blade. Only an expert can do that in such a professional way."

I thank him. Paul lightly shoves him aside. "Any idiot can do that! I, on the other hand, wrote your name on the stick."

I turn the stick to look at the side: AB HOFFMAN.

"If Muni had done it," says Paul, "he probably would have written your full name!"

"That's very nice. Thank you both," I say, moved by their kindness.

My father is holding my skates by the laces. "I did my

part. I sharpened your skates. I refuse to let some incompetent ruin the beginning of your career in the league."

My mother, who doesn't want to be left out, offers me the blue, white, and red jersey of the Canadiens.

"You can wear it at the neighborhood rink." She turns it over and shows me the back. I scream with joy. Above the number 6, she has glued the letters of my name: Ab Hoffman.

"Thank you everyone," I say, hugging them all; even my brothers who don't particularly fancy having their young sister's arms around their necks. Little Benny drowns us with wet kisses.

"Stop it!" screams Paul. "We're going to catch diseases!"

Then why is he hugging me even closer?

I know that he and Muni are happy for me, the tomboy of the Hoffman family. When my parents realized that I was so passionate about hockey, they never stopped me from playing. They never pushed me to do figure skating like some parents who encourage their daughters to wear tutus and white skates, and to put on make-up in order to be models of grace and femininity. But the Hoffman philosophy is: Hockey is a sport and sports are beneficial to our health. They are happy to see me healthy with a hockey stick in my hands because that's what I want!

Chapter 5

W'e're on our way to Varsity Arena—a fifteen-minute drive from our house. I'm in the back seat of the old blue truck, squeezed between Paul and Muni, with Little Benny on my lap. I'm in a prime position to listen to my brothers' stupidities.

"You know, Muni," says Paul, "if an opponent tries to insult Ab by shouting that he's playing like a girl, he'll actually be telling the truth."

Both of them crack up, of course. Even Dad is stifling laughter. My mother slaps him on the arm. "Don't encourage them."

"Mom!" I shout. "Stop it! Now is not the time to have an accident." My father has to be careful because it snowed last night. Not enough to close the schools (it's Saturday anyway), but enough to make the roads slippery.

"Yeah," says Paul. "Imagine the headlines: Two parents and their four boys injured in car accident. The girl is still missing!"

"One of the boys was protected by a jock," says Muni, still laughing.

"Jock jock!" Little Benny repeats.

POCK! POCK! His tiny fist just hit my jock twice.

"The witnesses heard tires screeching, metal crumpling and a curious…*POCK!*" continues Paul.

The boys are doubled over with laughter. I see my Dad's shoulders shake. Mom is hiding her face in her hands, surely from disgust…. No! She wipes the tears streaming down her cheeks. She's laughing so hard she's crying.

Finally, after what seems like an eternity, the building appears. Several cars are parked in the huge parking lot next to a side door, which must lead to the locker rooms. Boys in their hockey equipment, accompanied by their families, get out of every car; the fathers proudly carry the sticks, the sisters hang the skates around their necks, all under the eyes of beaming mothers.

But once again, we'll be the exception that proves the rule. In bright daylight, but unbeknownst to all, a Hoffman girl has joined the scene.

I try to stay calm, but it's not easy. My father and

my brothers wish me luck and head toward the arena's main entrance. My mother grabs the stick, and I carry the skates.

Mom is the knot specialist of the family, so she has been elected to make sure I can get my laces untangled for my first official hockey game. "You have to go to door number three," she reminds me.

Once inside the arena, we follow a narrow, barely lit hallway. How can two players wearing huge shoulder pads pass when they meet? Door number two is half-open. I glance inside. It's probably the team we're about to play. My heart beats faster. But I'm not nervous. After all, they're only boys. I'm just impatient.

We cross an open area that leads to the rink. The air is suddenly cooler. Off to the side, a man in a black hat and his sleeves rolled up sharpens skates. He rubs the blade back and forth on a grinding wheel that turns at breakneck speed, creating a shower of sparks.

Standing next to him is a boy my age—a redhead. He's fascinated by the movements that the man must repeat hundreds of times a week. The shrill blast of the referee's whistle turns my attention to a game unfolding in the rink. I sense, more than see the players. The boards are so high that only the tops of their heads are visible. I had pictured myself jumping the boards to get on the ice. I'll have to revise my plans. If I fell from this high up, I'd probably break a leg!

The sound of the puck hitting the boards, of blades carving through the ice, of the audience's screams, of the coaches' orders…I can't wait to be in the middle of all of this for real!

Mom touches my shoulder. "We should hurry, Abb…" She swallows the *ee* at the very last second. It would be silly, now that I've made it this far, to be discovered like that.

The redhead—the one whose skates are now sharpened—hurries past and unintentionally bumps me.

"Sorry." He takes off without another word and disappears into the locker room.

"Here's number three," says Mom. Just as we're about to enter, I see a warning written in chalk on a blackboard near the door: GIRLS FORBIDDEN.

What a beginning! By way of welcome, I could hardly ask for worse.

My mother looks somber. "You're not allowed to come in, Mom," I say apologetically.

She swiftly erases the warning with her sleeve. "The person who's going to stop me hasn't been born yet!"

Coach Al Grossi introduces himself. He's on the pudgy side; his bulk strains against his dark coat. A gray hat cocked slightly to the side, like those army berets that miraculously stay in place, rests on his head.

Mr. Grossi directs me to a corner of the locker room.

"You see, Ab? The number six hanging on the wall? That's your place."

I walk to my place confidently, my mother following behind me. I keep an eye out for inquisitive looks, but my presence hasn't raised an eyebrow. Everyone is busy tying their skates or talking to their neighbors. I don't know anyone in the group.

Mom hands me my skates. Her eyes are shining. She must be touched at seeing me living my dream. I hope she doesn't lose her cool in front of everyone. That would be too embarrassing.

"It's okay. I can untie the skates," I say to her under my breath.

She leans forward to...kiss me? I step back and quickly sit on the bench. I look at her with a mixture of annoyance and sadness. My mother can kiss me as much as she wants at home, but not here.

She immediately realizes her mistake and extends her hand instead. "Have fun, dau—"

No! Mom! No daughter here! I'm screaming at her in my head.

Panicked, my mother covers up her slip.

"Have fun, *SON!*" she says, raising her voice. She swings around and walks up to the coach. He gives her the regular season schedule. Then, without a glance in my direction, she steps out of the room.

"We're on the ice in ten minutes. Everybody, hurry up!" shouts Coach Grossi. To my right, a boy with thick black-framed glasses is staring at me. His father is at his feet.

"What?" I say, meeting his stare.

"You need your mommy to come with you to the locker room?" he says, mockingly. Pleased with himself, he hits his jock with his knuckles. *POCK!*

"Scotty Hynek," his father scolds.

I frown. "Maybe—but I don't need her to tie my skates!"

Score! And I too hit my jock. *POCK!*

A strange ripple effect follows. Automatically, all the boys hit their jocks as if to make sure the protection is in place.

POCK! POCK! POCK!

Goalie Graham Powell is sitting on a bench across from me. He needs the help of both his parents to strap his pads behind his calves, knees, and thighs. To my left, the redhead is yanking the lace of one of his skates. He pulls and pulls and…breaks it!

Stunned, he holds out the broken piece. "Oh, no!" he cries, on the verge of panic. "Not now! I don't have time to find my dad and get him to buy a new one!"

He tries to tie the two ends of the broken lace together but the result is disastrous. When he pulls, the knot comes apart. His laces are completely worn out.

The good thing about having brothers who played hockey before me is that I know these little problems can happen. I have an extra lace inside my hockey pants, just in case.

"Pull the lace out of your skate," I tell him. "I have what you need."

Scotty Hynek—the boy with the black glasses and the bad attitude—glances in my direction. But he doesn't seem to be looking at me. Very strange.

I give the redhead a new lace. "My name is Ab Hoffman."

"Thanks, Ab! If you were a girl, I'd kiss you!" he says with gratitude.

I'm so stunned, I'm speechless.

"I'm David Kurtis," he says.

"Five minutes!" calls Mr. Grossi. He just gave the parents who are still in the locker room their cue to exit.

I tie my skates quickly and elbow bespectacled Scotty in the ribs. "See? I can do this alone, like a big boy!"

And I emphasize the last two words.

David and I finish getting ready just as the coach starts giving his instructions. He lines up the offensive trios and pairs of defensemen. I'm happy to learn that I will play with David—him on the right, me on the left.

I still have to put on my Tee Pees jersey. But my pads always get caught in the back so I need help. I turn to David and then return the favor. Scotty Hynek makes a nasty remark. I choose to ignore it. That, of course, pisses him off.

Coach Grossi gives each player a sheet of paper that lists the ten golden rules of the sport. He asks that we become familiar with these rules before our first game. "I want you to make these rules yours."

"Assigned reading!" complains Scotty Hynek in a low voice. "We're not in school!"

Let's see what the ten golden rules are:

1) Play the game for the fun of playing.

2) Be generous when you win.

3) Be dignified when you lose.

4) Always be fair, whatever the price.

5) Obey the rules.

6) Work for the benefit of the entire team.

7) Graciously accept the decision of the officials.

8) Believe in the honesty of your opponents.

9) Behave with honor and dignity.

10) Recognize and applaud, honestly and wholeheartedly, your teammates' and opponents' efforts, with no regard to color, race, or beliefs.

I would add one more thing to this last line; gender. But so far, everything is going well. I'm one of the boys. A few of them seem agitated and nervous. I'm probably the only one to have a permanent smile on my face.

I'm still young, it's true—I'll be nine soon, on February 11th. But as I make my way to the rink, I'm about to realize one of the most cherished dreams of my short life. I couldn't be happier.

It's amazing what you learn about a hockey game when you're in the middle of it and not just watching from the bleachers.

First observation: I can keep up with boys my age. I don't lag behind or when I do, it's only for a few seconds. How could it be any other way? These boys are no different from the boys who play at the outdoor rink at home.

The games are short: three periods of ten minutes. The referee stops the game every two minutes to change lines. That way, no one is privileged because of his talent. When the game is over, everyone has played the same number of minutes. It's the principle of equality established by the Little Toronto Hockey League. Great idea!

We lost to the Hamilton Cubs by a score of 3-2. I wasn't on the ice for any of the goals.

Scotty—the guy with the glasses—is a real pain on the ice. He kept annoying the players on the other team.

One of them, Backstrom—a beefy guy who wears the number 9—didn't appreciate Scotty's comments about his size. During an attack in his zone, Backstrom body-checked Scotty and smashed him against the boards. Scotty lost his glasses.

A few minutes later, Backstrom found himself behind our net. I didn't hesitate for a second and threw myself at him. He fell sitting on the ice, slightly dazed. David recovered the puck and relaunched our attack.

Scotty—oh-so-grateful Scotty—approached me during the break, not to thank me, but to chew me out. "I could have taken care of this myself, Hoffman!"

"In your dreams, Scotty," I replied.

The beefy Number 9 got the upper hand again in third period. He hit the puck deep into our zone. I was about to intercept it when I felt his shadow next to me. I didn't have time to dodge him; he nearly flattened me against the boards.

In retaliation, my fellow defenseman, David, body-checked him. I recovered and was ready to show this bully what I was made of, but the referee stepped between us.

"You better keep your head up next time you come around, Backstrom!"

His answer was to ridicule me. "You play like a girl, Hoffman!"

David and I got penalties. So did Backstrom. Our opponents used their advantage to score the winning goal.

Jim Halliday and Russell Turnbull scored our team's two goals. They're by far the Tee Pees' best players.

After the game, our locker room is as quiet as can be expected after a loss. I'm convinced that Coach Grossi will let David and me have it. In fact, Scotty is happy to remind us of our mistakes.

"You made us lose!" he proclaims.

Red-faced from all his efforts behind the bench, Coach Grossi plants himself in front of us. "Take a lesson from David and Ab!"

"Yeah," Scotty pipes up, wiping the fog off his glasses. "They're the perfect example of what not to do."

"It would be easy to blame them for our loss," continues Mr. Grossi.

"Obviously," agrees Scotty.

David and I don't say a word. We untie our skates and put on our boots so we can leave the locker room as soon as possible. So much for Abby Hoffman's fabulous season...

The coach takes off his hat and wipes his sweaty bald head with a handkerchief. "These two deserve our..."

"...anger!" interrupts Scotty.

"...our respect!" Mr. Grossi corrects sharply. He paces up and down to make sure everyone is listening. "Yes, our respect. They came to the rescue of a teammate in difficulty, even if their opponent was bigger. That's the kind of team spirit I want for the Tee Pees. That's what I hope to see from all of you before the end of the season."

Coach Grossi raises a fist as a rallying sign. The players follow suit. "Tee Pees!" he shouts.

"Tee Peeeees!" we yell in response.

Relieved to not be scapegoats for this loss, but almost heroes instead, we go back to our places. David represses the urge to laugh.

"Coach," complains Scotty, "David and Ab are laughing at me!"

We all burst out laughing.

"You see what I mean?" he whines. "I'm going to tell my dad!"

Chapter 6

Sometimes my best friend exasperates me.

"I'm telling you, Susie. The players didn't shower after the game!"

She could have asked a thousand questions when we saw each other on Monday before the beginning of classes. Did I play well? Did I score? Was I nervous? Did I knock a guy against the boards? Did someone notice I was a girl pretending to be a boy? Did I use the toilet in the locker room? If so, did I pee sitting or standing?

But no! All Susie Read wants to know is what happened after the game.

My answer has the effect of a cold shower. Her enthusiasm about a feminine presence in a world exclusively reserved for boys drops a notch.

"It must not have smelled very good in the locker room," she says with a look of disgust.

"It smelled like defeat, Susie," I point out. "Not like sweat! Boys haven't started sweating at our age." In the same breath, I remind her that she can't tell anyone. And I mean it. "No one, Susie!"

"Why? What difference does it make?"

"It makes all the difference in the world! Isn't it obvious?"

If someone discovers my secret, I'm convinced I'll be expelled from the league. Despite our modern 1950s society, a girl playing hockey with boys is inconceivable.

The bell announces the end of recess. We return to class.

I'm still lost in my thoughts. Obviously, the battle won't be easy. That was made abundantly clear when I came out of the locker room after the game.

Bob Bowden, the coach of the opposing team, was on his way to see Coach Grossi. I was with my mother, who had come to pick me up. We bumped into Mr. Bowden in the hallway. He greeted my mother politely and pointing at me, said, "That *boy* of yours is quite the hockey player, Mrs. Hoffman."

He emphasized the word *boy*, then winked and smiled before catching up with his friend Al. My stomach was in a knot. *He knows!*

I remembered that my brother Muni is friends with Mr. Bowden's son. I bet that big mouth told him that his little sister plays hockey with boys.

Mr. Bowden was in a good mood. His team had just won its first game. But what will happen next time if his team loses? And if I score the winning goal? Will he complain to the chairman of the league that there's an impostor in the game? Do I have to remain unnoticed on my own team, like half of the players whose names or faces I don't remember? At least that way, I wouldn't attract unwanted attention.

Will he reveal my identity to Coach Grossi?

I share my worries with Susie. She's absorbed in an arithmetic problem. "Hey, Abby, this is complicated…"

"Thank you for understanding."

"Understanding what?" she says, chewing on the pencil's eraser. "I'm having a hard time solving problem number four. All these divisions, it's really complicated."

"Hey! We're talking about hockey, not about math!" I'm upset with her.

"Oh." She apologizes. "In figure skating, it's much simpler. If a boy wants to pretend to be a girl, everyone will know right away."

Ms. Morley puts an end to our conversation.

"Abigail and Susie, keep your comments to yourselves…"

The thought of my brothers, or Bespectacled Scotty, in pink tutus makes me smile.

At dinner on Monday night, Muni confirms my fears. He confesses that he might have talked about me to Bowden Junior.

"I only told him my brother Ab plays for the Tee Pees."

The shock makes me drop my fork on my plate. Little Benny immediately imitates me.

My mother jumps in: "But your friend is well aware that you don't have a brother named Ab!"

"He'll figure it out for sure," says Dad.

Muni tries to defend himself. "Is it my fault that he's intelligent?"

I'm boiling mad. "I wish I could say the same about you, Muni!"

"Mom, at home is it Ab or Abby?" he asks.

"Abby," she answers, surprised by his question.

He sticks his tongue out at me.

"Abby, baby!" he shoots.

"Abby, baby! Abby, baby!" echoes Little Benny.

Paul is surprisingly quiet. He's hardly looked up from his meal during all this. He seems absorbed by the contents of his plate. I throw a green pea at him.

"Abby! Don't play with your food!" Mom warns.

"Mom, he's hiding something, I'm sure of it!"

"Paul told his friends too," Muni confides, happy to shift the attention away from himself. My older brother swallows his last piece of beef with difficulty.

"Me? Well…"

"Yes! Yes!" continues Muni. "I heard you at school!"

Paul avoids my eyes and tries to stay calm. It's no use, his cheeks turn bright red. "Well…I mentioned it to Erica Westbrook. I…I wanted to impress her," he explains.

"I thought your only passion was rocks, Paul," notes Muni. "Are you doing a different kind of research?"

Paul is more and more interested in the opposite sex, these days. He is fifteen, after all. But is he so desperate, or so helpless, that he needs his little sister's achievements to start a conversation with a girl?

"Paul has a girlfriend! Paul has a girlfriend!" Little Benny and I chant to tease him.

My father smiles. But my mother is not happy with the news.

"She's not my girlfriend!" protests Paul. "At least, not yet…"

The two met at the Young Naturalists Club of Toronto. My mother points a finger at Paul. "You should concentrate on your studies instead of chasing girls!" Then she turns to her husband. "And you, Samuel H. Hoffman. You need to have a man-to-man conversation with your son about the facts of life…"

My father and Paul have the same reaction: "Oh, no!"

The expression they have on their faces! It's so funny that my mother, Muni, and I crack up. It breaks the tension that was threatening to ruin the evening just a few minutes ago.

"Seriously, guys," says Dad, in a calm voice. "You shouldn't spread Abby's story. Let's keep this between us, okay?"

"The least people know, the better it will be!" adds Mom. "If your sister's real identity is discovered, I'm afraid she'll be expelled from the league."

"Not everyone would agree with the fact that a girl can play hockey with boys," continues Dad. "Most people believe that when girls put on skates, it should be for figure skating and nothing else."

Paul and Muni take a minute to think. At the same time!

"What should we do about the boys we already told?" asks Paul.

"The boys and *girls*," notes Mom.

"There's only one girl," he replies.

"Tell them the truth," suggests Dad. "They should understand Abby's position."

My brothers agree with a nod.

My mother puts her hands on the table in front of her.

"Now, Paul, let's talk about this Erica Westbrook."

The night before the second game of my career, there was no getting-up-in-the-middle-of-the-night prank. My parents had warned my brothers.

But once again I didn't sleep well; I was too excited at the idea of playing hockey. And worried that the news would spread and I would be betrayed in the locker room. At 3:10 a.m., that's a guaranteed nightmare for sure.

To take my mind off this growing fear, I storm into my brothers' bedroom, shake Paul, and rip off his blankets.

"Hurry up, Paul! You're late for your date!"

He opens an eye. "Wh...what?"

I shake him again. This is fun. "Hurry up! Your date with Erica Westbrook! She's waiting for you in her father's car!"

The key word is Erica. As soon as he hears that name, Paul leaps out of bed and flies out of the room. Incapable of thinking straight, the only concepts that register in his primal brain at this early hour are Erica Westbrook and late. Probably in that order. He crosses the kitchen, grabs his coat from the hall closet, and rushes out into the night.

I switch off the lights and lock the door. From the living room window, I watch my big brother stand in the cold night, in pajamas, at the edge of the yard.

"What are you doing, Abby?" says Muni in a sleepy voice. He's dragging his feet across the floor. He's not really awake.

"Shhh! I'm watching Paul. He's outside, kissing his Erica Westbrook."

A spark lights Muni's eyes. "You might be able to spy on them from behind the garage. Less than a minute ago, he was holding her in his arms."

Muni is already delighted. "Hee! Hee! Hee! Brilliant idea, Abby!"

He throws on his coat, quietly steps out and hugs the wall of the garage to sneak up on his brother.

Once again, I lock the door. Suddenly aware of the situation, Muni goes to Paul. There's no Erica Westbrook on the horizon. Only an Abby, waving at them from the kitchen's bay window, enjoying her sweet revenge.

"Good night, guys!"

My brothers run to the front door. I run too—but in the opposite direction to my bedroom. I lunge for my bed and pull the blanket over my head. Heavy pounding rattles the door, and then the sound of the bell pierces the night.

I hear angry steps—my father's—in the kitchen. Lights come on. A voice flares up: "What are you doing outside at this hour?"

Mumbled excuses. A stifled laugh—mine. Paul won't reveal that he thought Erica Westbrook was waiting for him. And Muni will be too embarrassed to explain that he was spying on his brother.

But most of all, my brothers' pride will prevent them from telling my father that their evil little sister yanked their chain.

I feel lighter, as if I've just scored three goals in the finals for the Stanley Cup! My anxiety is gone.

Chapter 7

Going early to Varsity Arena is a good idea. Even if we hit a traffic jam we won't be late. We had to pull Little Benny and my two big brothers out of bed. Paul and Muni were snoring like freight trains, except an octave higher. My parents were not about to leave them alone at home, sleeping like hibernating bears.

"They were up doing crazy things in the middle of the night," Mom told my father. Paul and Muni were silent. They never accused me of having pulled a prank on them. They knew it was fair game.

In the parking lot of the arena, I tell my mother I don't want her to take me to the locker room. I don't want Scotty to make fun of me. Plus, I'm old enough to lace up my skates. That's all I have to do; I'm already wearing the rest of my equipment, including the St. Catharines Tee Pees jersey.

I flinch when my mother leans in to kiss me on the cheek. From the corner of my eye, I just spotted three boys—our opponents for today—wearing the blue Marlboros jerseys. As they pass me, one of them give me a little shove with his shoulder.

"Get out of my way, you mama's boy!" he spits out. It makes his friends laugh.

I can tell by my mother's eyes what she's going to do. I plant myself in front of her as she's about to lunge at the brat, grab him by the ear—the right one, her favorite—and force him to apologize.

"It's okay, Mom. His turn will come once we get on the ice." I make note of his number: 8.

It takes everything I have to convince my mother to let it go. "I'd better not see his parents in the bleachers or they'll get a piece of my mind!" she says.

"As long as you don't scream my name at him, Mom."

She walks away to catch up with her husband and sons, and I enter the building through the door reserved for the players. It's still early. I have half an hour in front of me.

When I cross the open area leading to the rink, I hear music. It's a Strauss waltz: *The Blue Danube*. I can play it on the piano. There are no pucks hitting the boards, and no parents screaming to encourage their kids or to criticize the referee.

Figure skaters have taken over the rink. I move a little closer to take a look. Sitting on the players' bench, I see two dozen girls in uniform. They spin like tops, jump like toads, fall on their bottoms and cry like babies.

Oh! There's Susie Read, looking like she's in control of her movements. She glides on one leg, like...uh...like a pink flamingo. Her arms are stretched out to keep her balance or maybe so she can fly off.

As soon as she spots me, she skates over. "Hey, Abby! It's nice of you to come and see me skate!"

I give her a dark look. "No Abby here, Susie!" I whisper.

She quickly apologizes and corrects herself: "It's nice of you to come and see me skate, AB!"

That's better. I relax.

"Your sport is a little short on pucks," I say, watching the skaters.

A voice behind me grates on my ears. "Is that your girlfriend, Ab-ominable?" I don't have to turn around to know that Scotty has arrived.

Susie bursts out laughing. "Me, your girlfriend?"

"Are you going to kiss her, Ab-erration?" he says, mockingly.

"It's just Ab, Scotty!"

"Yeah, but Ab is not a name. It's only the first two

letters of the alphabet. We can do what we want with it."
And then, with a smirk, he adds, "Unless you prefer...
Abigail!"

I try my best to keep a straight face. Does he know?
Or did he pick a girl's name at random to tease me?
Offence is the best defense: "Do you know the difference
between a salamander and a chameleon, Scotty?"

He thinks for a moment before giving up.

Susie is my witness. "In the end, Eve Lismer was
right about a scrawl in boys' brains."

Now here comes Muni with an odd smile on his
face. He nods toward Scotty.

"Is that your boyfriend?"

No! Not again!

Ticked off, Scotty turns to Muni. "Who are you
talking to?"

That's when my dumb brother realizes his blunder.
He just broadcast that I could be Scotty's girlfriend—me,
Ab Hoffman, a hockey player pretending to be a boy.

I stare at my brother. How do we get out of this? It's
Susie who ends up saving the day. Both for me and for
Muni!

"Scotty? My boyfriend? Are you kidding?" says Susie,
her cheeks turning bright crimson.

Scotty is all too happy to side with her. "Me? Her
boyfriend? Are you kidding?" he repeats.

Phew! Scotty has had the wool pulled over his eyes.

Since we're standing side-by-side, Muni could just as well have been talking to Susie. Strangely, Scotty didn't look at Susie. He barely even glanced at her. That's odd. I could swear Scotty's eyes are crossed. But they looked okay a few seconds ago.

"Oh! I guess I made a mistake," says Muni, without apologizing. Then he turns to me and asks, with an exaggerated wink, "Hey, Ab. Is Susie *your* girlfriend?"

Faking disgust, I answer him. "That? My girlfriend? You can't be serious!"

I turn on my heel and head to the locker room. Scotty follows me, leaving Muni and Susie behind. I can hear Susie's angry voice:

"THAT? I'm a *that*? I'll show you what a *that* is, Ab Hoffman! You're the most useless boy I've ever met!"

My best friend is not only a good figure skater, she's a great comedian!

●

I hate the Toronto Marlboros!

They're really brutes. I don't think they're my age. I suspect some of them shaved before the game so we wouldn't notice their beards! One of the players is as big and tall as my brother Paul! David Kurtis is the Tee Pees' most imposing player and he only comes up to the guy's eye level.

During the game, some of our players are downright

frightened. If the puck is shot into the corner or near the boards, they avoid going after it.

"You guys—stop dragging your butts!" barks Coach Grossi, furious at his team.

If only the Marlboros were just bums on skates... but no! They know how to play. After two periods, we're behind 5-1. Our goalie, Graham Powell, is bombarded from all sides. He can't perform miracles all by himself. On top of that, that pain in the neck who wears number 8 crashed into Powell at the top of first period. He's the same one who shoved me with his shoulder outside the arena. His name is Hodge. He's their right winger. He's quick on his skates and always in motion—like a pesky fly. And he's just as hard to catch. I tried twice to get him against the boards but at the last second, he deked and I took the hit and cut my cheek on the boards.

I left the game, my glove covering the bleeding injury. My mother rushed to the players' bench. I was showing my cut to the coach, but when he saw my mother, he sent me to her.

"You still need your mommy, Ab," Scotty sniggered. "For what? You have a big booboo, big baby?"

I took the glove from my face. "For this!" I said, my cheek still gushing blood.

It's as if the lights went out in Scotty's head. When he saw the blood, he turned white and passed out behind the bench.

"Great! Another one gone!" the coach exclaimed.

My mother examined my cheek. She wiped off the blood with a damp towel and put on a bandage she fished out of her purse. "You should be able to finish the game without staining your jersey." I could tell she was upset because of my injury.

"Not now, Mom!" I whispered.

A first scar thanks to—not because of—a hockey game is like a badge of honor. For me, it's as important as a goal. I wasn't about to let my mother seal it with a kiss. It would have been *so* embarrassing.

I took my place next to Scotty, who had come back to his senses and was showing a little more color.

"It's not fair! I want a war wound too!" he grumbled, envious.

"Well, you have to *go* to war for that, Scotty. Not run across the ice trying to flee the enemy!" I tell him.

The Marlboros don't slow down in the third period, even though they secured victory with a fifth goal in the middle of the second. Their intention is clear: they want to humiliate us.

We step up our efforts with little result. We manage to limit our opponents to one more goal, but we don't succeed in slipping one past their goalie.

I'm very competitive so it makes me mad that the game is sliding away and I haven't been able to give

Hodge—the number 8 Marlie—a taste of his own medicine.

Every time he skates by our bench, he shouts: "Hey, Tee Pees! You play like girls!"

There's not much time left in the game. I take a sip of water. Paul once explained that I shouldn't drink too much during a game otherwise I might get a stomach ache. Usually when we're on the bench, we spit out the water at our feet. The guys on the St. Catharines Tee Pees—our junior hockey team—do that during games.

Once doesn't make it a habit—I spit out the water toward the ice. Supreme coincidence, Hodge happens to be there exactly at that moment. I'm such a goofball!

His mouth is open because he's about to insult us again, so he gets a snootful. He barrels toward our bench, his eyes popping out of his head, and raises his stick to hit us. The referee steps in and throws him out of the game for unsportsmanlike behavior.

"But he spit in my face," Hodge protests.

The referee interrogates our coach.

"I didn't see anything," Coach Grossi replies, shrugging.

"It was Hoffman, Sir," claims Scotty, moving away from me. *What a snitch!*

Captain Jim Halliday steps in.

"No, it wasn't Ab, it was me..."

David Kurtis, my partner, on the blue line, also comes to my rescue. "No! I'm the guilty one!"

"Liar! It was me!" asserts Russell Turnbull.

For the sake of fairness since an offence has been committed, the referee chooses to expel one of the Tee Pees from the game.

"The first one to lay blame is often the offender," he declares.

He points to Scotty and blows his whistle. "You!"

"I'll tell my dad," whines Scotty as he heads to the locker room.

The Hodge incident strengthened the bonds of our team, the coach said after the game. I'm not proud of how it was done but between you and me, I'm happy with the result. In hockey, as in life, you have to command respect.

"Hurrah for Ab Hoffman!" shouts our captain.

"Hoffman? But I'm the one who got sacrificed," reminds Scotty, offended.

His comment is met with general indifference. My teammates surround me and congratulate me.

Chapter 8

These days, when the phone rings after dinner in the Hoffman house, it's usually for Paul. When he starts speaking in a low voice, we know his beloved Erica Westbrook is on the other end of the line.

Tonight the phone hasn't finished its first ring before Paul has beaten everyone and picked up. It's almost seven o'clock. I sit close by and pretend to look at a scrapbook of the best female athletes of the 1920s and '30s, put together by my mother when she was young. She collected newspaper articles about the heroes of her time. I stop on the page dedicated to runner Bobby Rosenfeld, who won a gold medal in the 400-meter relay race at the 1928 Olympics in Amsterdam.

"It's for me," says Paul, trying to move away from me, which is impossible because the cord isn't long enough.

"I like this girl," says Mom while working on the household budget, a pile of papers spread across the kitchen table. "It's good for girls to call boys instead of waiting by the phone the boys to call them."

My father grunts in agreement. He's busy washing his white lab coat in the sink. He sprays stain remover on the edges of the sleeves, which got dirty in the chemistry lab at Canadian Industries Limited where he works.

"Mom, your scrapbook is very interesting," I say, eavesdropping on Paul and Erica's conversation.

"Thank you, Abby. Make sure you read the article about Myrtle Cook."

"I will."

Paul presses the receiver against his ear and shields his mouth, hoping to be heard only by his girlfriend. It's no use—I'm all ears.

"Hello, Beautiful," he says in a suave voice. "How are…"

He hands me the phone, embarrassed. "Abby, it's for you. It's your coach."

My parents look up and glare at Paul.

"What's wrong?" asks my brother. *The idiot…Abby… My coach….*

Paul drops the receiver as if it has suddenly become red hot. The receiver dangles at the end of its cord, bumping against the counter a few times.

"Hello? Is someone there?" asks a male voice from the receiver.

I recognize the voice of Mr. Grossi, to whom Paul has just whispered sweet nothings *and* revealed my true name.

With a sharp gesture, my mother urges me to answer. Okay, but how do I get myself out of this? Inspired, my father abandons his laundry and whispers a solution in my ear.

I grab the phone.

"Hello, Ab? Why did your brother call you Abby?" the coach asks. "That's a girl's name, isn't it?"

I swallow hard. I have to make this good. "Oh, that? It's just a stupid joke between brothers. We tease each other by giving each other names that end with the sound 'ee.' In the family, we already have Muni and Little Benny. So for him, I'm Abby. Right Pauli?"

My brother makes a face and walks away. He signals to me to keep the conversation short because he's waiting for a call from his Erica. I pout. I hope Mr. Grossi has plenty to say.

"Well! I called to let you know about a change in the schedule. Saturday's game will be at 1:00 p.m. instead of 2:00 p.m. We're playing the Hamilton Cubs. Have a good evening, Ab…ee!"

Relieved, I reply: "You too, Al…ee!"

He laughs and I hang up. Phew! That was close!

Almost immediately, the phone rings again. I pick up before Paul can get to it. With a wicked grin, I hand the receiver to my brother. "It's for you, Pauli dear."

I should be in a good mood. Today is Sunday so I don't have to go to school. Last night at Varsity Arena, the Tee Pees won their first game of the season 4-2 against the Hamilton Cubs.

I didn't accumulate any points, but on the other hand, I wasn't on the ice when our opponents scored. I also blocked two shots with my pads, one of which was heading for the empty net after our goalie fell down. When the puck hit my leg, it really hurt. It hit the side of my calf—which isn't protected by equipment.

I collapsed on the ice because of the pain. It felt like I had been kicked viciously.

The referee stopped the game, and I was escorted to the bench by my blue line partner, David Kurtis, and captain Jim Halliday. Scotty, who was hanging nearby, moved away when it came time to help.

"You're delaying the game!" he complained.

The pain was so intense, I could hardly hold back the tears. I didn't want to alarm my parents and have my mother hurry down the bleachers to come to my rescue. I knew that would be her reaction so I waved to reassure her.

I skipped one shift, hoping a short resting period would make the pain go away. I wasn't entirely steady on my skates when I went back on the ice, but in the heat of the game, I found my groove again. Anyway I had no choice; a Cubs player slipped between David and me and flew toward the net.

"He's your man, Ab!" shouted Coach Grossi.

In plain language that meant if the player made it to our goalie alone, I would be blamed. I skated like crazy to catch up with him and lifted his stick before he could shoot. The puck slowly glided toward Graham Powell, who stopped it with his glove.

We were at the end of third period and the score was 3-2 in our favor. One goal from the Cubs and we would have had to settle for a tie. There's nothing exciting about a tie, Mr. Grossi once told us before a game. It's a little like kissing your sister.

"Yuk!" was the Tee Pees' response. I made sure I joined the chorus.

I was happy to have blocked the Cubs' attack. Almost as much as if I had scored my first goal. The coach showed his appreciation by giving me a formidable slap on the back after I returned to the bench. On the next play, since the game was coming to an end, Hamilton pulled its goalie. Our captain put the puck in the net with a precise shot from the centerline, and we celebrated the first victory of our young season.

After the game, Jim Halliday didn't retire to our locker room. He stayed on the ice with the three captains of the other Little Toronto Hockey League teams: Bobby McGuinn from the Toronto Marlboros; Bob Canning from the Hamilton Cubs; and Fred Stanfield from the St. Michael's Majors.

The four players had been picked by their coaches to symbolize the first National Hockey Week, organized by the Canadian Amateur Hockey Association. To help promote the event in the papers, the boys stand behind a large banner that reads: Let's Help Our Boys Become Better Men!

That hit me hard. Doesn't anyone realize that hockey could also help girls become better women?

The puck from the game against the Cubs was given to Jim Halliday, our captain, who scored two goals, including the winning one. A good sport, he gave it to goalie Powell who also played a great game. Then Powell came to me and put it in my glove.

"You earned it, Ab," he said.

Scotty, sitting next to me, expressed his impatience. "Come on! Stop giving it to just anyone!"

"Would you like to have it?" I asked.

"What kind of question is that?" he replied, his eyes popping behind his glasses. "Is the sky blue? Will the Toronto Leafs win the Stanley Cup? Are guys better than girls in everything? It's a given!"

I took a deep breath to calm myself down. Scotty is an acquired taste. "You're right, Scotty," I admitted. "We can't give the puck to just anyone."

"Thanks, Hoffman!" he answered, extending his hand.

I got up. "That's why I'm returning it to our captain."

I have all the reason in the world to be happy: first victory, no school. Then why am I not in a better mood? Because of a five-letter word that cannot be uttered in my presence. A terrible word to someone like me.

When the puck hit my calf, I held back tears of pain. But I'm sure not holding back these tears of anger.

"There will be no discussion," says Mom. "Period!"

Humiliated, I'm forced to put on...a dress! That's the hateful five-letter word.

It's horrible—I always wear jeans!

The reason for this disguise is brunch out with my grandparents—my father's parents—who are rather stuffy. My other grandmother wouldn't care a bit what I was wearing. But my Hoffman grandparents can't stand the fact that my mother kept her first and last name, Dorothy Medhurst, after marrying their son; they think she should be Mrs. Samuel Hoffman! Having the soul of an artist and teaching art to kids doesn't help their relationship with my mom either. They don't approve of her career.

I don't try to hide my frustration. "It's like forcing Paul or Muni or Little Benny to wear a dress! I don't want to!"

My mother finally calms me down. "Pick your fights, Abby," she advises. "Is wearing a dress worth this waste of time and energy and tears? Plus, we're going to talk about Christmas gifts."

My mother has a way of coming up with the perfect arguments to defuse the bomb I was threatening to become. And I have to say, she's not crazy about wearing dresses all the time either.

My father, meanwhile, makes sure he has the agreement of his sons. There will be no teasing; otherwise the Christmas gift list will be shortened.

I reluctantly put on the one thing from my closet that serves as a dress: my Brownie uniform. I have a feeling my friend Susie has dozens of dresses—one for every occasion—hanging in her bedroom closet.

As soon as my brothers see me, they swing around and bury their faces in their hands. Only Little Benny comes toward me, delighted.

"Pretty Abby!"

"Yeah," I say, with a forced smile.

It's truly Abby today.

My long black coat hides my dress but it doesn't protect the bottom of my legs. It's cold and dry outside.

Once at our destination, we hurry into the restaurant. My grandparents—Albert and Divine Hoffman—are seated at a large round table in the back corner of the room. My grandfather is adjusting the horrible wig on his head. It looks like a mop without the handle. He gets confirmation from his wife that everything is in place. The restaurant—a popular hangout after the eleven o'clock Sunday church service—is busy this afternoon, and the conversations are lively.

After the greetings, we take our places around the table—me, between Paul and Muni, facing my grand-mother; Little Benny near his grandfather.

"Your hair is very short, Abby," notes my grand-mother, disapprovingly. "It's a good thing you're wearing a dress otherwise you'd look like a boy."

"Thank you for the compliment, Divine."

"Grandmother," she corrects, her lips pinched together.

I force a smile and remind myself that I want a new pair of hockey stockings for Christmas—mine have holes in the knees. My grandfather, seeing that the girls' conversation has started, addresses my older brothers.

"So, guys. The hockey season is going well?"

"Yes," says Paul.

"Yes," says Muni.

"Yes," I say, quickly abandoning the conversation with my grandmother.

My grandfather's blue-gray eyes sparkle behind his glasses. People in my family say that I have his eyes.

"Boys, you're lucky to have your little sister's support at your hockey games," he says in a kindly way.

"Actually, the opposite is also true," remarks Mom. She obviously isn't interested in talking fashion with her mother-in-law.

"Meaning?" asks my grandfather, perplexed.

"That Abby plays hockey with boys," reveals Dad.

My grandparents are so shocked that there's a moment of utter silence. Little Benny grabs the opportunity to snatch the wig off my grandfather's head and, with a giggle, put it on his own head.

Paul and Muni burst out laughing. My mother, laughing too, removes the hairpiece from Benny and gives it back to its owner. My grandfather, not at all offended, puts it away in his wife's purse.

"*What* did you say, Samuel?" asks my grandmother.

My father very patiently repeats what he just said. He recounts the events surrounding my registration, and describes my first games in the league with the Tee Pees. Had we told my grandmother that I had just enrolled in the army, she wouldn't have been more stunned.

"But…Abby…you're…a *girl*!" she remarks, scandalized.

"You have very good eyes, Grandmother Divine," I say, with a hint of sarcasm.

"Girls figure skate, they don't play hockey!" she adds.

"Is this true, Samuel?" asks my grandfather.

My father, whose attitude I highly appreciate, doesn't try to hide or even disguise the truth. In fact, he's amused by his parents' reaction. Not me. I find them mostly annoying.

"Only boys can play hockey, right, Paul and Muni?" asks my grandmother, looking for support. My big brothers shrug and stay silent, not wanting to compromise their chances of getting Christmas presents.

"No, you're wrong!" interjects Mom. "Sports are good for boys *and* for girls. And hockey is a sport, my dear Divine!"

"Mrs. Albert Hoffman," she corrects. She turns to her husband: "See, Albert, the bad influence she has on her daughter!"

In other circumstances, my grandmother's comment would have caused an explosion at the table. But not today. We have to pick our battles, Mom said this morning. Reasoning with her mother-in-law is not on her list of priorities for the day. In fact, she gave that up a long time ago.

My grandfather, who has recovered from the surprise, now has a wide grin on his face. "Abby plays hockey with boys? Why not? That's wonderful!" He lowers his voice as if he were sharing a secret. "And no one knows?"

"No one," I say, happy to have him on my side.

He makes me promise to call and let him know when the next game at Varsity Arena will be. "We want to go see you play," he says. "Right, Divine?"

My grandmother stares at the menu.

"That means yes in grandmother speech. She has a lot of catching up to do to be of her time," my grandfather translates. Then, he signals for the waiter who immediately comes to our table. "We're ready to order. Put everything on one bill, I'm paying. We're celebrating today!"

"Something in particular?" asks the waiter.

My grandfather points to me with his chin. "My granddaughter here plays hockey!"

So much for being discreet...Let's blame that on an overflow of enthusiasm.

The man looks like he has just heard a very bad joke. He replies with a snicker:

"Sir, it's not very feminine for a girl to play a rough sport like hockey! May I have your order, please? I'm very busy."

And don't have a lot of time to waste listening to non-sense. He didn't say it, but that was clearly what he meant. What an idiot! I hope my grandfather doesn't give him a big tip.

"It's true!" whispers my grandmother, in a tearful voice.

A burst of laughter coming from another part of the restaurant makes me look up. A family reunion like mine. Ordinary. I imagine the conversations and...*No! Nooooo!*

There, among the group, is a familiar redhead: David Kurtis, my blue line partner!

I must have a grim expression because Paul notices. "Abby, why are you so pale? You look like you just saw a ghost!"

As a matter of fact, I would rather have seen a ghost right now than one of my teammates. I hide the side of my face with my hands and, in a low voice, explain the situation to my parents. "If David sees me dressed as a girl, it's over for me!"

"But you *are* a girl, Abby!" notes my grandmother, on the verge of despair.

"Until further notice, she's no longer Abby," Dad announces to the whole table.

"She's Ab," Muni adds for my grandparents' benefit. "That's her boy's name."

Needless to say, my grandmother is completely overwhelmed by the turn of events.

"Hide under here for the rest of the meal!" suggests Paul holding up the tablecloth.

"Great idea! I'll take your pancakes," says Muni, already salivating at the idea of having a mountain of pancakes on his plate.

"No!" Mom interjects calmly. "We have to make an intelligent decision, but quickly because our table is right next to the bathroom. Sooner or later, your friend will come this way."

I've lost my appetite. My stomach hurts. Out of all the restaurants in Toronto, why did the Kurtis family choose this one? Or why didn't my grandparents suggest we meet somewhere else? And what if I hadn't listened to my mother? If I had put on a pair of pants, like I wanted, instead of this stupid dress, bumping into David wouldn't be an issue.

Paul looks over my shoulder. "Abby, I don't want to alarm you but I think he saw you...He's getting up."

My heart races in my chest. *An idea, someone!*

My mother orders Muni and me to follow her to the bathroom. "But my eggs are going to get cold," whines Muni.

"No discussion!" replies Mom in a tone that doesn't leave room for discussion. My brother obeys. He and I scurry after her toward the bathroom.

Just in time! When I close the door, David is by our table.

A moment later, we emerge. David is still talking to Paul. I greet my teammate. My father is amused but my grandparents are dumbfounded.

"Hi, David!"

"Hi, Ab," he says. "I thought I saw you from across the room."

I squirm in clothes that are too big for me, trying my best not to show my embarrassment. Good manners require that I introduce David to my family.

"You and Ab are a great pair of defensemen," compliments Dad.

"Thank you, Mr. Hoffman," David replies. "Ab makes it very easy. He has an instinct for hockey."

"Good grief!" mutters my grandmother.

"And this is my brother, Little Benny."

To distract him and make sure he doesn't spill the beans, even though he barely speaks yet, my grandfather has lent him his wig. Little Benny is playing at putting it on and off his head.

"Maybe this would be a good Christmas present for Benny!" my grandfather jokes.

Finally, I indicate the person standing next to me. "And this is…uh…my sister, Muni…"

"Munie with an 'e'," specifies Paul, not daring to look at our brother for fear he'll explode with laughter.

"Hi, Munie. Uh…nice dress," David says.

Muni stares at him.

My teammate is uneasy. The silence that follows doesn't help. "Well…I should go back to my parents' table. See you next Saturday?" He politely excuses himself and leaves.

I take my seat, and the tension leaves my body. My appetite is back. I attack the mountain of pancakes sitting on my plate.

"No, these are mine!" declares Muni, squeezed into my Brownie uniform.

My mother had to be very persuasive in that bathroom. Muni finally capitulated. Given the urgency of the situation, he had little negotiating power. "Doing a favor for your sister is not asking for much," said Mom.

Luckily for me, but unluckily for him, Muni is only a little taller than me. That's why we were able to trade clothes so easily. But in the tight quarters of a bathroom stall, it was less hassle for me to slip on his pants than for him to squeeze into my dress.

For obvious reasons, we don't linger at the restaurant. My parents invite my grandparents to have dessert at home.

"Is that where you'll announce that Muni has taken up figure skating?" asks my grandmother with hint of sarcasm.

The waiter brings change to my grandfather and reluctantly thanks him—the tip was proportional to the value of his opinions. His eyes rest on Muni. "Is she the one who plays hockey?" he asks arrogantly.

"Yes! And she's very good," I say, defiant.

We head toward the exit. On the way, I say good-bye to David Kurtis and his family. His parents seem more intrigued by my strange older sister than by me.

While we're retrieving our coats from the coat check, another group of customers enters. Now it's Muni's turn to turn as white as a sheet.

His best friend Bowden Junior is in front of him...
And he recognizes Muni.

Chapter 9

Luckily for Muni and me, we can count on Bowden Junior's silence. A good friend, he promises to forget the dress episode and the fact that a girl plays hockey in a boys' league.

Despite the humiliation, there's something positive in this for my brother. He has a new appreciation of what I have to go through. "Girls should never wear dresses in the winter. It's too cold for the legs," he complains after we get back home.

Paul reminds him of the consequences of his disguise. "If you want to go to Abby's games, you'll have to wear her dress again, in case David is there. Right, Mom?"

I don't dare add anything.

My mother reassures Muni. "You're not meant to wear a dress, my son," she says.

"Neither am I!" I say, taking a few dance steps, comfortable in my pants. I don't need much to be happy: a pair of pants instead of a dress, boys to jostle with instead of girls to chat with (except for my friend Susie Read), skates on my feet instead of winter boots, and a hockey stick in my hand instead of a dishcloth.

When those conditions are met, I'm in the best of all worlds. After putting up with wearing a dress for too many long hours, nothing makes me happier than to play hockey with the Tee Pees the following Saturday. The game is in the early evening, at five o'clock.

We're playing the St. Michael's Majors.

With my enthusiastic way of playing, it was bound to happen sooner or later. A penalty. I'm always willing to jump into the fray, even if it means a few more bruises on my body. Opponents who venture into our zone must be willing to pay the price. I never miss a chance to hit the puck, let alone a player.

A Majors forward at my blue line dekes to the right before veering abruptly to the left.

Number 14, Fred Stanfield, slides the puck between my skates. Thrown off balance, I hold on to him. He falls. The referee blows his whistle.

"Number six from the Tee Pees. Two minutes for tripping," he announces.

"I didn't even touch him!" I plead in vain.

I look toward my bench to make it clear that the referee can't see straight, like all referees. Coach Grossi remains impassive. With a gesture, he tells me to serve my sentence. I don't argue. Some players are as excited to get a penalty as they are to score a goal. Not me! There's nothing glorious or honorable about sitting on the penalty bench. It's really…a penalty! Like when my mother sends me to my room.

Scotty skates toward me. To cheer me up? When pigs fly!

"Way to go, Hoffman! Creating problems for us…"

He swings around to get in position for the faceoff. I drift slowly toward the penalty bench. What a strange feeling! I'm watching my team play with a man short and I can't do anything. Even worse—I am the cause of it.

The two minutes on the bench are the longest since my start with the Tee Pees. The game is tied 2-2 and I feel totally useless. Our goalie, Graham Powell, saves the day more than once. At times, when their forwards are buzzing around our net, I stare at the floor, dreading the cheers from the crowd that will indicate St. Michael's has scored. Then the tension lowers, a sign that the Tee Pees have managed to push back the enemy and clear their zone.

The man in charge of the scoreboard—who is sitting next to me—has to tell me that it is time to jump back on the ice.

In junior hockey, I'm always impressed to see the players jump the boards when leaving the penalty bench. It's amazing. Impossible for me to do. The boards are so high, I would break my neck.

I waste precious seconds trying to open the door. However, my late return on the ice turns out to be a break; the action has moved into our zone. The puck is shot across the centerline—directly onto the blade of my stick.

So here I am, barrelling toward the opposing net. I hear the crowd cheer me on or…maybe cheer on the enemy defenseman. I cross the Majors' blue line. I am about fifty feet from the goalie.

I have to think fast. Shoot or deke? I glance at the goalie; he is so huge that it's almost as if the net has shrunk! There's no room for the puck.

Too bad! I hit a wrist shot toward the goalie's glove. When I play with my brother Paul in the net, that's my strategy. He has a hard time catching the puck…I hope the same is true for the Majors goalie. But the puck hits his stick and rolls into the corner.

Missed!

From the bleachers behind the net, I hear my brother Paul shout: "She almost scored!"

My parents shush him. Paul covers his mouth with his hands.

While the players from both teams, forwards and defense, are coming back into St. Michael's zone, I find myself—me, a defenseman—in an unusual position: behind the opposing net.

I catch a glimpse of center Russell Turnbull, stationed in front of the net, just as a defenseman throws himself at me. I can see in his eyes that he isn't after the puck. He's after me.

Bespectacled Scotty is screaming at the top of his lungs on the red faceoff circle.

"Here, Hoffman! Here!" he keeps shouting, his stick pointing toward the ceiling.

The trouble is that he's surrounded by two Majors forwards. If I pass the puck to him, chances are it will be intercepted. I opt to shoot the puck in front of the net, betting on Turnbull's chances to retrieve it. At the same time, I narrowly escaped the enemy defenseman charging at me. He looks like he wants to rip my head off. I hear a shout coming from the bleachers behind me. Paul again. A furious Paul. A blunder-prone Paul…

"Hey, Fox!" (that was the name of the Majors player.) "Don't you lay a hand on my sis…"

The rest gets lost in the cheers celebrating Turnbull's goal. He put Coach Grossi's advice into practice: "Keep your stick on the ice. You increase your chances of hitting the puck."

Scotty has a hard time with this concept.

As soon as Turnbull received the puck, he slid it between the goalie's pads. His goal gives us the lead, 3-2. Thrilled with his feat, he raises his glove before coming to congratulate me.

"Nice pass, Ab!" he says, ruffling my hair.

Our teammates join in. They hug me as if I were the one who has scored. Scotty congratulates Turnbull, then criticizes me as we're going back to the bench.

"I was open, Hoffman! You should have passed the puck to me."

Even on the bench, Scotty continues to complain. "Of course, Mr. Hoffman wants to score before I do. Mr. Hoffman would rather pass the puck to the team's best scorer than to his other teammates."

I wish I could tell him that his "Mr." is music to my ears.

The voice of the announcer resonates throughout Varsity Arena. "The Tee Pees' goal was scored by number 16, Russell Turnbull! With an assist from number 6, Ab Hoffman..."

Hearing my name like that fills me with pride. My first point. But it makes Scotty angrier.

"See, Hoffman? See? He should have said: The Tee Pees' goal was scored by Scotty Hynek!" He pauses, a jealous expression on his face, and adds: "With no assist!"

"Good job, Ab!" says Coach Grossi, slapping me on the back.

He leans over Scotty's shoulder and whispers: "Keep your stick on the ice if you want your teammates to pass to you."

I see Scotty's ears turn bright red, but I don't say anything.

"Stop laughing, Hoffman!" he barks with his teeth clenched. "I can hear you all the way from here!"

We win 4-2. David Kurtis scores the last goal with an unintentional assist from Scotty Hynek. Toward the end of the game, Scotty tries to fire a clearing shot toward the boards. The puck must have hit a bump in the boards because instead of continuing on its course, it bounces to the center of our zone, directly onto David's stick. My partner shoots the puck to the other end of the rink, into the net deserted by the Majors in favor of another forward.

The siren announces the end of the game. We all gather around our goalie to celebrate our accomplishment.

"Did you see my nice pass, Hoffman? Did you see?" Scotty is full of himself. I hit him in the shoulder, which makes him wobble on his skates.

"You anticipated the trajectory, right, Scotty?"

"Of course! Good thing it was David and not you who got the pass. You would have shot in our own net instead of St. Michael's net...."

Why do I waste my time with this guy?

Back in our locker room, the atmosphere is cheerful. Only one face is somber: Scotty's!

"What's the problem?" asks David Kurtis.

"It's not fair!" Scotty grumbles. "No one announced your goal and MY assist!"

Jim Halliday, who overheard the conversation, decides to address the situation. He asks for silence in the room. "Gentlemen, I must immediately correct an injustice committed against two of us." He clears his throat and in a loud voice, imitates the announcer.

"The Tee Pees' goal was scored by number 4: David Kurtis!"

The Tee Pees scream and bang their sticks on the floor. The sound is deafening. Sitting next to me, his jersey still on, David enjoys the show.

Captain Halliday waits a few seconds for the room to quiet down. Coach Grossi looks on approvingly as Halliday continues: "With an assist from..."

He lingers a bit. To my right, Scotty is so impatient to hear his name said out loud for the first time that he's literally bursting out of his skin. Noticing Halliday's hesitation, he stands up and turns his back to him to remind him of his number.

"11! Number 11!" he whispers.

The captain reacts: "With as assist from...the BOARDS!"

The Tee Pees crack up. Not Scotty, of course. I catch Jim's attention with a nod and indicate he shouldn't drag this on for too long.

Halliday pulls himself together and finishes the announcement. "And from number 11: Scotty Hynek!"

I bang my stick on the floor and cheer for this player who earned his first point in regular season play. The others follow suit. Jim Halliday goes back to his place while Scotty waves to his teammates, like an emperor to his devoted subjects...Once he's sat back down, he shoots:

"Not too jealous, Hoffman?"

"You bet, I am!" I laugh.

My smile quickly disappears when Coach Grossi announces the team's next meeting. "Saturday morning, eight o'clock. But not at Varsity Arena...at the hospital."

Scotty explodes. "At the hospital? Are you crazy?"

Mr. Grossi ignores the question. He continues, "for a complete medical exam..."

Oops! I didn't count on this....

Chapter 10

"It's not in my contract," complains Scotty.

And yet, apparently it is…in our contracts. Well, let's be clear on the term contract. We don't get a penny in exchange for our talents and services as hockey players. We even have to pay 25 cents for every game. But it was on the Little Toronto Hockey League registration form, written in tiny characters: an "invitation," more like a command, to go through…*a medical exam* during the year.

"The league wants to make sure kids don't suffer heart attacks in the middle of a game," Coach Grossi explained during a phone call on Friday night.

The medical exam is scheduled for Saturday morning at the hospital. All the players, without exception, must go through it or they'll be asked to leave the team. Once the exam is done, a doctor will issue a certificate of good health. No certificate, no hockey.

Not knowing what might be in store for me, my parents accompany me to the hospital. At around eight o'clock, dozens of young people are already waiting in a large room. Schedules had been drawn up. From 8:30 to 9:30 a.m., players in our category—eleven and younger—will go through a series of tests to evaluate their physical condition.

The chairman of the league, Earl Graham, is directing traffic. After handing us a form to be filled by a doctor or a nurse, he divides us into groups according to alphabetical order. H for Hoffman, group 2, which also includes two other Tee Pees: Scotty Hynek—oh great!—and the captain, Jim Halliday.

I also recognize Hodge from the Toronto Marlboros in this group. The Marlies are easy to spot; they're wearing their team jerseys. Hodge looks terrified and is holding his mother's hand.

My brothers have to go through this too, but later in the afternoon.

"Mom, what are they going to do to us?" I'm worried. My mother glances at my form.

"A complete medical exam…" she reads, emphasizing the word "complete." She rolls her eyes and whispers a few words in my father's ear.

"I have a few people to talk to, Ab," she explains before leaving.

My group is called to another room to begin the tests. I leave my jacket with my father. I'm trying not to worry too much. Standing in line next to me, Scotty is even more nervous than usual.

"This medical exam thing is totally unfair!" He holds out the form and shakes it, "I don't need a test to tell me whether I'm healthy or not. I know! Why don't I sign the form myself and get out of here!"

"You're going to sign it in cursive or print it?"

A man in a white lab coat, with a stethoscope around his neck, tells us to get undressed.

"It doesn't matter," continues Scotty, pushing the glasses up his nose. "A doctor's signature is always just a scribble."

I don't listen to him. After a minute, the man's instruction finally hits Scotty. "What?" he asks, frightened. "We have to be naked?"

He dashes for the exit. "No hockey game is worth me showing my butt to everyone!"

I feel like following him. Except I really like playing hockey!

Jim Halliday, who is…in his underwear, catches up with Scotty. I look away. It's suddenly very hot in the room. "Nobody will be naked, Scotty," promises Halliday. "We keep our underwear on."

No player is more relieved to hear that than me. Not even Scotty, who is now getting undressed. Hodge objects: he wants to keep his Marlboros jersey on. His request is denied.

I try to be discreet so nobody will notice me. I'm the only girl in a roomful of boys wearing nothing but undershirts and underpants. I'm holding my clothes in front of me at waist level, like a screen; my pants are folded in half and fall down to my knees. I can't let my…difference show.

I have to stay calm. Easier said than done—my heart is pounding. Someone behind me pushes me in the back. I spin around and grab him by the collar of his shirt.

"Keep your distance!"

Scotty pulls my arm. "Come, Hoffman! I don't want to suffer alone."

We walk down a cold hallway. There are no windows to the outside, only rooms with open doors. Curious as a cat, I peer into one of the rooms. I see a boy in a wheelchair. He's only slightly older than me. When he sees me, his face lights up and he waves. I smile and wave back. Suddenly, having to go through a medical exam doesn't seem like such a big deal. There are worse things in life.

"I hope they won't keep us for the night," whispers Scotty. "I didn't bring my blankie or my teddy bear."

Coach Grossi is standing by one door. He lets us into a large room in groups of four. His face is red.

Tightly squeezed into a three-piece suit, he's breathing with difficulty.

"And the doctors are worried about us?" remarks Scotty. "They should take a look at the adults."

I enter the room with Jim Halliday, Scotty, and another player I don't know. Boys—about ten at a time—are doing different tests. It's a sort of circuit that starts on the left, stretches along the wall, and continues all the way to the exit. Scotty is directly in front of me. He offers me his place—a suspicious offer that I politely decline.

"What, Hoffman, are you scared?" he says.

With a quick glance, I take in what's going on. Nothing too complicated, it seems. Only one test has me perplexed. The boys disappear behind a curtain; after I hear them cough, they reappear with a strange look on their faces—a mix of happiness because it's over, and embarrassment for reasons I don't understand.

Next to me, a boy hastily gets dressed. He shows everyone his certificate of good health. "I got it! I got it!"

"I'll give you two dollars for it," pleads Scotty.

Too late. A plump nurse instructs him to follow her. At the same time, she indicates that I must leave my clothes on a chair. I don't like that at all. I feel even more vulnerable than when I play hockey without a jock.

"Next!" calls the nurse.

It's my turn. I hand her my form, which she quickly reads. "Your name is Ab Hoffman, is that it, my boy?"

"Yes, Sir," I say before realizing my mistake—must be the deep voice and the budding moustache—and correcting it: "Yes, Ma'am…"

"We're off to a good start," she grumbles. "I don't look like a man anymore than you look like a girl."

Without ceremony, she makes me stand in front of a wall with a height chart. She writes down my height: four feet three inches. Then she tells me to step on a scale. She manipulates the weights until the rod is perfectly balanced.

"You weigh 67 pounds, my boy…"

She shows me where to go next. I join Scotty, who is sitting on a chair, waiting. "I'm three pounds heavier than you, Hoffman," he gloats.

"It's because of your glasses!"

Our stops at the next stations go reasonably well. No big deal. People examine our throats and ears, listen to our hearts—mine is beating more regularly now—and lungs, check the reflexes at our elbows and knees. But when we get to the eye test, the situation becomes more complicated…for Scotty.

He comes up with an excuse to let me go first. I read the letters on the eye chart hanging a few feet away from me, from the biggest to the smallest, with both eyes first, then with only the right eye, and finally with only the left eye.

Between my reading sessions, I observe Scotty. He

seems terribly anxious; he keeps wiping his hands on his thighs. When his turn comes, he sits on the stool.

"Both eyes," instructs the attendant in a dull voice.

Scotty reads very slowly, which irritates the adult.

"Can you pick up the pace? We don't have all day."

It sounds like he's reciting a multiplication table, as if he wanted to learn it by heart. Then he covers his right eye with his hand and repeats the exercise, with identical results. But when comes time to cover his left eye, he goes into overdrive. "E-F-P-L-P-E-D-P-E-Z-F-D-E-D-F-C-Z-P-D-E-F-P-O-T-E-C."

Surprised, the attendant asks him to read again but more slowly. This upsets Scotty. "What do you want? Am I too fast or not fast enough?" he complains with reason. "I passed the test, right, Hoffman?"

He read so fast that I must have missed some letters, but all in all, he can see just fine.

The boys next to us are growing impatient. There aren't enough chairs for them. This station is experiencing a backlog.

Without waiting for instructions, Scotty covers his...right eye and reads the chart again with disconcerting ease. He's cheating but the attendant doesn't notice.

The boys clap, as if trying to chase him from the stool.

"All right," grumbles the attendant, handing Scotty his form.

Scotty catches up with me at the last station. Ignoring all good manners, he makes me change seats. In doing so, he goes back to his original position, the one he had when we first arrived. Two boys are waiting next to the closed curtain. It's strange because all of the other tests are happening out in the open.

A slight cough is heard behind the curtain. "Everything is in order," says a man. The two boys exchange an embarrassed look.

"When you have to cough, you have to cough," says the next boy in line. The curtain parts on a kid all too happy to get out of there; he's earned his certificate of good health.

"Good-bye, son!" says the attendant—a mountain of a man—while wrapping a huge arm around the next boy's shoulders. If he's not careful, he might break him in two! He leads the boy inside the station and closes the curtain.

"What team do you play for?"

The answer is lost in the questions that Scotty fires to his immediate neighbor. "Cough? Why cough? I don't have a cold!"

The boy is short of breath, an obvious sign of anxiety. "The doctor makes us cough to make sure we have two…" He swallows with difficulty. "Telling him is not enough. He has to check for himself…with his hand."

"Two? Two what?" asks Scotty.

Had he said that the Earth was flat, the boy wouldn't have been more stunned.

"Well…two…you know…" He discreetly points to his lower abdomen.

"Two…"

Oh, no!! I finally get it. The difference…I'm toast! Coughing my lungs out won't save me! Impossible for me to escape. If I run away, no matter for what reason, I won't get my certificate.

Another cough…

The curtain parts.

"Next! What team do you play for?"

The only ones left are Scotty and I, sitting on chairs, and three boys standing in line. Scotty feels his arms, his legs, his eyes, his ears, his shoulders…"Two…I have two of everything! Why do I have to be examined behind a curtain?"

He still doesn't get it. Exasperated, I say: "Under your jock!"

Instinctively, he goes to hit the protective shell. His fist stops in mid-air. "Two," he repeats, incredulous.

Light coughing is heard beyond the curtains. Scotty starts to shake. What if I run away now? But where? To the bathroom? The boys' or the girls'? If I don't get my certificate, there's no point. A volunteer standing by the door is collecting the forms. He makes sure all the tests have been done, otherwise he sends the player back to the appropriate station. I would have to give up my hockey season. But if my secret is discovered, the outcome will be the same anyway.

I feel my eyes well up with tears. Tears of anger. It's so unfair! To be a girl in a world of boys is not a disease. I'm in very good shape. And no doctor can tell me otherwise!

Whatever will be, will be, I guess. Doctors are intelligent. They should be able to understand my situation.

Strangely, Scotty seems calmer. "It's just something unpleasant to get through," he says to convince himself. "I have to handle this like a man, not like a girl."

"Next!" calls the doctor as he opens the…

"Aaaaaaah! It's his turn! It's Hoffman's turn!" shouts Scotty, in a panic.

I'm so taken by surprise that I can't come up with a reply. I can hardly breathe when the doctor wraps his arm around my shoulders.

"What team do you play for?"

In the small area behind the curtains, the only furniture is a chair and a stretcher. "Lie on your back, Ab," he instructs me while glancing at my form.

I choose to remain standing. I have to explain everything, reveal everything. And quickly, so the boys waiting for their turn won't become suspicious. I'm convinced that Scotty is hanging around to see my reaction to the exam.

"Doctor, I…I have something to tell you…"

"Oh?" says the doctor. "Something I haven't heard yet today?"

"Yes…I…"

A voice—a woman's voice—comes from the other side of the curtain.

"Doctor McMillan?"

"Yes?"

He opens the curtain. A lady with an engaging smile hands him a file. "Your patient, Mr. Oxford, is acting up again. If you wouldn't mind taking care of him."

Doctor McMillan sighs.

"And the boys' tests?" he says, as if he were looking for an excuse to avoid Mr. Oxford.

"I'll take care of them until you come back."

It takes me a few seconds to realize my luck.

"Should I finish with this one first?" suggests the doctor, talking about me.

Absolutely not!

The lady's smile disappears. "YOUR patient threw his food tray in the nurse's face," she replies.

The doctor grabs the file from her and exits. I don't know why but the attitude of this woman doctor makes me want to trust her. She closes the curtains, frowns and looks at my form.

In a pretend authoritative tone, she orders: "Cough, Ab Hoffman!"

Do I need to say that I'm still standing next to her and that she has her arms crossed over her chest?

I happily obey.

She waits a few seconds, her eyes smiling, and declares: "Two! Yes, perfect!"

The doctor, whose name I don't know, hands me my completed form. She leans toward me and whispers: "I wish you a fabulous season, Abby Hoffman! I'm Dr. Thériault, a friend of your mother…Dorothy is my daughter's kindergarten teacher."

I'm overcome with relief! I finally have my certificate of good health, signed by Dr. Thériault.

Before leaving, I try to get my act together. After all, I can't look like I just won the Stanley Cup! That's not the kind of reaction this type of test is supposed to trigger. I try not to smile. The doctor winks at me, and then puts on a stern expression. She opens the curtain.

"Next!" she says to Scotty. The presence of a woman doctor for this final exam frightens the boys. Scotty rebels:

"No! I want the real doctor!"

Despite the insult, Dr. Thériault doesn't lose her cool.

"Come on, I've tamed wilder beasts than you."

"Tamed?" Scotty squeaks.

"If you don't come right away," threatens Dr. Thériault, "I won't sign your form and your hockey season will be over."

"Scotty! Do this...like a man!" I say to encourage him.

Like a prisoner sentenced to death, Scotty goes behind the curtain.

"You want to know which team I play for?" whines Scotty.

"No," says the doctor as she closes the curtain. "Cough!"

"Atchoo!" Scotty replies.

"Oh! You have a cold," diagnoses Dr. Thériault. "I just happen to have suppositories for that..."

"Aaaaaaah!"

Chapter II

Some games in my season will go down in history, at least in my little history, but not necessarily for the right reasons.

If only I could have scored my first goal in a one-goal win against the hateful Toronto Marlboros on this Saturday, February 11th—my birthday—it would have been perfect.

In my dreams!

The harsh reality is that the Marlies did us no favors. A setback, 4-1. Our only goal was scored by center Russell Turnbull.

It was a difficult game. The Toronto forwards kept getting through our defense. I found myself out of position more than once. But thanks to our goalie, we didn't have to suffer a more humiliating loss. With only a few minutes left to play, I tried to block a wrist shot from a Marlboros player. The puck hit my left ankle. I let out a yelp and collapsed on the ice. Two teammates had to help me to the bench.

Once in the locker room, my mother showed up. "I don't think it's broken, but we should go to the hospital to make sure."

She helped me take off my other skate and we left for the hospital. My mother was right; my ankle wasn't broken. But to give myself a chance to fully recover, I had to use crutches for a while.

So that's my little story.

In the context of hockey, walking on crutches is quite a badge of honor. It's a little like getting a war injury, but one that doesn't prevent you from going back to the front. At school, it's an entirely different story.

How will I explain what happened to my classmates? I don't want to walk without my crutches; I need to be fully recovered before the weekend so I won't miss a game. I confess that I consider telling a white lie: I sprained my ankle by slipping on a sheet of ice. This kind of accident happens all the time, especially to older people.

When I arrive at school, in a car no less, I make a huge splash. If Scotty had been around, he would have peed his pants.

Susie Read rushes toward me. "Hey, Abby. What happened to you?"

I quickly tell her the truth before a mob of curious onlookers surrounds us.

"Abby was hit by a puck," says Susie. So much for slipping on a sheet of ice. Her explanation is met with surprise and disbelief.

"What? You play hockey, Abby Hoffman?" says a boy, with contempt.

"Girls don't play hockey," adds another one in the same tone.

"Why not?" objects a girl with long blonde hair. "What stops girls from playing hockey?"

"Their dolls!" a boy scoffs.

Then all eyes turn to me. I still haven't answered the question. The kids are hanging on my every word. I could pretend that Susie misunderstood, and that I hurt my ankle because I slipped.

But I see hope in the girl's eyes. If I lie, I'll disappoint her. But if I tell the truth, I'm putting myself in a difficult position. Knowing that I play hockey in a boys' league, some nasty person could tell on me to the directors of the Little Toronto Hockey League. My career would be over.

I opt for a half-truth.

"I do play hockey! I played on Saturday at the rink in front of my house."

"The rink at Humberside Collegiate? Impossible!"

says a boy. "I spent the whole afternoon there and I didn't see you."

This guy doesn't intimidate me.

"Duh! I play hockey in the evening, with the older boys, when you're in bed with your teddy bear!"

That shuts him up. "The puck hit my ankle during one of the games."

"It was...it was her brother who hit it, right, Abby?" Susie feels compelled to add, already regretting to have put me on such thin ice.

"Yes!" I say, frowning for her benefit. "Muni hit a wrist shot that bounced off the side of my ankle."

"And he was very sorry about it," insists Susie. I hit her in the leg with my crutch. No need to overdo it.

"But he didn't lose sleep over it!"

The girl with the long blonde hair smiles at me. She offers to carry my heavy school bag to my classroom. I thank her, and give it to Susie instead.

"That'll keep you busy."

While I make my way through the crowd, I hear the boys talk among themselves.

"If it were me, I wouldn't need crutches."

"See, that proves that girls can't play hockey."

And again...

"Girls should stick to figure skating. Hockey is a sport for guys!"

Stupid guy talk!

After two days, I give up the crutches. I can walk comfortably enough, and put weight on my ankle without too much pain. The swelling has not completely gone down yet, but my mother is taking care of it with her ice treatments.

By Wednesday evening, I'm dying to slip on my skates and test my ankle at the rink in front of our house. My mother is going out of her mind trying to convince me that it's too early. Seeing I won't give up, she finally suggests I put on my skates and see for myself.

As soon as I tie the laces, I feel a sharp pain in my ankle.

"Wait a bit," she advises. "It'll be better tomorrow night."

"But I want to play hockey!" I say, frustrated.

"It's better to miss one night than to miss an entire week, isn't it?" reasons Dad.

Tomorrow is Thursday—two days before our next game. I spend the long evening practicing piano and reading and head for bed early to make the time go faster. In bed, I keep feeling my ankle to test the degree of swelling and my tolerance to pain. The night is endless. I barely sleep.

Morning brings disappointment. When I put on my boots, my ankle feels tender.

"So, Abby…how's the ankle?" asks Dad.

"It's fine. I don't feel anything."

I bet that grown-up players like George Armstrong, Maurice Richard, and Gordie Howe have jumped on the ice even when they were injured. They overcame the pain so they could play. Well, I can suffer for my sport too. I just have to clench my teeth and give it my all, like my idols.

I was careful all day, but by evening the swelling has barely gone down. I can put on my skate, but if I tie the laces, I get a throbbing pain. Will I be fully recovered for Saturday's game? The season is so short. I can't afford to miss a single one.

Friday afternoon, after school, I have to know once and for all. I have to put my ankle through the test at the Humberside rink.

I slip on my skate and tie it without too much problem. Once on the ice, I skate comfortably enough. But I'm not going to overdo it.

Paul is playing hockey with his friends. He suggests I wait before joining the group. "If your ankle isn't healed, you'll make it worse."

So I'm skating in the section reserved for girls, the section where figure skating rules. I'm bored. Going around in circles quickly becomes monotonous. *To hell with it!* I cross the gate that divides the two sections and I'm back in familiar terrain: hockey. A player takes off on a breakaway. I block him, steal the puck and pass it to a forward.

"Hey, Abby! You're on my team," says Jack Adams, surprised.

It's my turn to be surprised.

"We made up the teams while you were skating with the girls," he explains. "Paul knew you would join us before long."

My ankle! I don't feel any pain!

I want to scream with joy. But first, I rush to guard my goalie, Paul, at the other end of the rink.

"Go, Abby! Go!" my brother yells.

Chapter 12

My ankle held up, thank goodness, but not my toes...

"It's shrinking cold!" Scotty is next to me, shivering on the players' bench.

"Yeah, we need warmer socks," I say, my teeth chattering.

"What?"

Scotty doesn't seem to know what I'm talking about. *Did I say something stupid?*

Scotty hits his jock. *POCK!*

"Shrinking," he says.

Obeying some kind of masculine reflex, the other Tee Pees on the bench imitate him.

POCK! POCK! POCK!

Even the referee who is watching the game nearby hits his jock.

POCK!

Not wanting to be outdone or to make anyone suspicious, I do the same.

POCK!

I'm embarrassed. I must be turning bright red. Now I understand Scotty's reaction when I suggested warmer socks.

"It was a joke!" I say to justify myself.

The air from my mouth comes into contact with the cold air of Varsity Arena and creates condensation. We look like a team of smokers.

The building has been transformed into a giant refrigerator. The heating system is broken. The temperature outside is frigid, so you can imagine how cold it is inside. The bleachers are almost empty. The few spectators are trying to keep warm by drinking coffee after coffee.

Actually, the worst things for the players are the toes. They're crammed inside tight skates that don't protect from the cold. Even one or two pairs of wool socks don't make a difference. To try to maintain circulation in our feet, we walk on the spot. Both teams have adopted this makeshift solution. It creates a strange background noise, like a small army marching with steel boots.

It doesn't really work, but at least it keeps our minds off the problem.

In the heat of the game when we're on the ice, there's no time to dwell on these details. For my part, I'm just happy my ankle is holding up. My only fear is that a puck will hit my frozen toes. They'll fall off for sure.

Because of the cold, the players get permission from their coaches to wear their tuques. I'm wearing my Montreal Canadiens tuque. It used to belong to Muni, who got it from Paul. My parents believe if the item is still in good condition, there's no reason to waste money on a new one.

Scotty Hynek is wearing a leather hat with earflaps. However, his problem is not with his head but his moon-shaped face: his glasses. When he breathes, the warm air fogs them up. He can't see a thing.

"There's fog on the ice," he complains.

Then there's another problem—a serious one for the person concerned, but funny to everyone else—the referee's whistle. The referee's *metal* whistle.

When Lefty Gardiner raises his arm (the left, of course) to call a penalty, the whistle sticks to his lips. He tries to act cool, but he can't get it unstuck.

It's so funny that for a few seconds, we forget about our frozen toes. Every time the poor man tries to speak, inhale or exhale, he starts to whistle. Because the situation is distracting the players, he sends the two teams back to their respective locker rooms.

The rooms are heated so no one complains. We take off our skates and slip our feet into our warm boots as fast as we can. But our toes don't thaw out quickly. The process is very slow and very painful and generates a lot of moaning, gritting of teeth, and tears.

There is no conversation during this forced break. Only Scotty's howls when the stick of his neighbor to the right falls on his foot.

And to think that in a few minutes, we'll have to go back into the arena! There are two more periods to play— that means our toes will freeze again. But this time, we all know what to expect when we retire to the locker room.

Someone knocks on the door. It's Lefty Gardiner, the referee. He has freed himself from the whistle, as evidenced by the red mark across his lips. He looks like he just put on lipstick.

He tells us that he won't use the whistle during the game anymore. He'll ring a bell. "So pay attention to what happens on the ice," warns Lefty. "Good luck!"

A new rule is established. Rather than the usual two-minute shift on the ice, our playing time is shortened to one minute. That way, we spend less time waiting for our turn and suffering.

I love playing hockey, but the rest of the game is really difficult. In the heat of the moment we forget about our toes, but the return to the bench is also a return to the harsh and cold reality. Yet sometimes funny things happen.

"Hey, guys! Look!" shouts Jim Halliday. He inhales deeply and his nostrils stick together, as if an invisible hand were pinching his nose. His teammates on the bench imitate him. It doesn't warm us up, but it does make us laugh!

Except Scotty, who panics. "I can't breathe!" he screams, his nostrils stuck together. "I can't breathe!"

"Open your mouth, Scotty," Jim replies, bringing on another round of laughter.

The outcome of the game against the Majors becomes clear in the third period. Our forward Russell Turnbull hits with lightning speed. Seconds after faceoff, left of the opposing goalie, he sweeps the puck toward the net. Surprised or frozen, the goalie doesn't have time to react and Turnbull's shot slides between his pads.

We play the last five minutes very mechanically. Everyone is distracted. Lefty Gardiner only rings the bell for offsides; he doesn't give penalties anymore. Let's get this over with seems to be his goal.

When the siren confirms our victory 3-2 over the Majors, the players from both teams hurry to the locker rooms. But a few minutes are not going to make much difference to my frozen toes. So, along with a few other die-hards like Jim Halliday, David Kurtis, and Russell Turnbull, I go to congratulate our goalie, Graham Powell.

Graham is not moving. He's crouched in his usual position to block shots. But there's no one shooting. He doesn't react to our presence; he just continues to stare at the empty space in front of him.

"I think he's frozen in place," says Russell, who bravely removes his glove to touch Graham's face.

"Let's push him to the locker room," suggests Jim, stepping behind his goalie.

David and I grab Graham's arms and lead him to our locker room so he can come back to life. He's like a mannequin in a department store window. Maybe if he had received more shots on goal in the third period, he wouldn't have frozen. Or at least, we would have realized an ice statue was guarding our net.

The return to the locker room has an air of *déjà vu*. It's a repeat of the first forced break. The toes are thawing and so is Graham Powell.

Does the fact that we won soften the pain? Hardly. But at least, we didn't suffer for nothing.

Coach Grossi's ears, not at all protected by his gentleman's hat, are bright red. He congratulates us for our courage and reminds us of our standings—three wins and four losses. The regular season is well underway and we're in second position, behind the Toronto Marlboros and ahead of the Hamilton Cubs.

"I want to let you know there will be a league all-star game on March 23rd. The players chosen to represent the

Tee Pees will be contacted this week."

Oddly, the coach looks in my direction.

"I've been selected, Hoffman," whispers Scotty. "He winked at me."

"You have a great imagination," I tell him.

"You're jealous," he replies.

Suddenly, what I see astonishes me. "Scotty...your right eye..."

"What?" he asks, anxious.

"Your right eye is not looking in the same direction as the other one."

His left eye is staring at me, but the right one is stuck...looking at the ceiling!

He quickly hides his face and runs to the bathroom. He comes back a few minutes later and takes his seat. "What were you saying, Hoffman?" he asks, trying to sound casual.

"That your eye was not looking..."

Scotty opens his eyes extra wide. "Looking where?" he asks, impatient.

Everything is back to normal. "Uh...I was wrong...I thought your right eye was frozen."

"Optical illusion," he replies with a shrug. "It's your brain that's frozen, Hoffman!"

The game scheduled for Saturday, February 25th is cancelled because of a horrible snowstorm. We can't tell the ground from the sky. The match is rescheduled for March 3rd.

The possibility of playing in the league all-star game is not even on my mind. I haven't scored a single goal this season. I got two assists and four penalties. My mother gives me money when I score a goal or get an assist. Clearly, I haven't struck gold in my first year with the St. Catharines Tee Pees.

There are only two games left in the regular season. Though I did my best on the ice, I didn't make an exceptional contribution like Jim Halliday, Russell Turnbull, or Graham Powell. They are the ones who are responsible for most of our victories. Without these three, the Tee Pees would sit in fourth place, at the bottom of the rankings.

So I have no illusion as to my chances of being considered among the best players of the league. Yet when the coach kept looking at me at the end of the last game, it seemed meaningful. Or was he looking at my partner, David Kurtis, or worse…at Scotty Hynek?

Scotty, a star? When pigs fly!

The weather has warmed up. On Monday night, I play hockey in the rink in front of my house for a couple of hours and come home to go to bed. As soon as I step into the living room, my parents break the news.

"Abby, Coach Grossi called earlier," starts Dad.

My heart skips a beat. I feel the excitement rise in my chest, even though I'm trying hard to stay calm. It doesn't even occur to me to take off my jacket and tuque.

"To give us the new schedule?" I ask in a neutral tone.

"Yes," answers Mom. "I wrote it down." She hands me a sheet of paper. The playoffs start on March 16th. We're playing a yet-to-be-determined team based on the rankings of the regular season. My mother also noted down the all-star game of March 23rd, which she circled in red. Several exclamation marks followed.

"There was something else," says Dad, his eyes sparkling.

Paul and Muni, who arrived home shortly after me, move in closer, intrigued.

"What is it?"

My mother locks eyes with me. "Abby, you've been selected for the all-star team!"

My disbelief immediately turns to joy. Paul and Muni are so thrilled that they lift me up on their shoulders for a lap of honor around the house.

"Here comes the Star of all Stars: Ab Hoffman!" shouts Paul.

Once the hero of the day—that's me—has landed back on the floor, my parents give me a great big hug. Ha! If I had Scotty's phone number, I would call him just to rub it in. I've always believed girls could play hockey as well as boys. The fact that I'm on the all-star team of my league—and not just in a pickup team at the Humberside rink—is certainly proof.

I'm so excited. But something in my parents' attitude tells me I haven't heard the whole story yet. Even my brothers notice.

"Is there a problem, Mom?" asks Muni.

The silence that follows confirms that indeed, there is.

"Okay," I say, unnerved. "I'm part of the all-star team. But...what? Am I a substitute? Or the mascot?"

My mother looks very serious. "To make sure all the players belong to the same age category, the authorities ask that the players provide their birth certificates—"

"And?" Muni tries to understand.

My father seems upset. I don't quite grasp the implications of this request. "And?" Dad continues. "On Abby's birth certificate is her full name...and her gender..."

F...for Female.

I feel the ground cave beneath my feet!

SECOND PERIOD

From February 27, 1956 to March 11, 1956

Chapter 13

It's the journalist's last question. I feel the eye of the camera focused on me. But I've been warned to not look directly into it, to act as if it doesn't exist. It's difficult with these bright spotlights everywhere. They make me squint and throw a blinding light on the ice of Varsity Arena.

"So, Ab, what do you think of all this attention?" he asks.

I answer with a smile. "It's complete nonsense!"

The journalist waits a few seconds.

"Got it!" says a voice behind the camera. Then the man bursts out laughing.

"You're so right, Ab!"

My mother, who is going to be interviewed later, joins us. So does Al Grossi, who will also be part of this television news segment.

"I swear, Ab, it's as if you've done interviews like this all your life!" exclaims the journalist. "I've met Maple Leafs players who were incapable of expressing an opinion without hesitating."

The cameraman, who has turned off the spotlights, adds his two cents worth.

"Maybe we should ask the little boy to give lessons to the professionals." He laughs at his own joke.

"She's a little girl, Teddy," says the journalist with a sigh.

I wish I could have said that this whole thing was pure madness. But after discussing it with my mother a few minutes before the interview, she helped me understand that "nonsense" better described what's been happening over the last few days.

For sure it is nonsense to forbid a girl to play hockey like boys, or even with boys! I'm living proof of that.

Nonsense: something that defies common sense and reason. I thought madness was just as good. But apparently on television, you have to watch what you say.

"The segment will be broadcast on Friday night during the six o'clock news."

"We don't have a television," I tell the journalist.

"Now *that's* complete nonsense!" declares Teddy.

I don't bother to tell him that our family owns a cottage near a lake, north of Toronto, that has no running water or electricity…and it's magnificent!

"But we have hundreds of books," says Mom.

"Now that's madness!" replies Teddy.

Nonsense…madness…That's what's been happening since Al Grossi's call.

I can't believe the news. I have all the reasons in the world to be thrilled. After all, I've been selected for the all-star team. But in order to be on the team, I have to provide my birth certificate…which carries my full name and gender.

There's a strange calm in the air. We're all aware of the stakes. Even Little Benny, who usually babbles from dusk to dawn, is playing quietly with mini-bricks.

"What if we forgot to send the certificate?" suggests Muni.

"Or what if it got lost in the mail? These things happen," adds Paul.

"It wouldn't change the outcome. Abby wouldn't be able to play," replies Dad.

"The player and his parents are responsible for providing the birth certificate," notes Mom. "Mr. Grossi was definite—no certificate, no all-star game." She picks up Little Benny who is asking for a hug. Then she addresses my father, even though I'm the one concerned. "What if we simply send them Abby's certificate?"

My father thinks out loud. "With a little luck, no one will notice that our Abby is different. Just like last November, on the night of the registration..."

"Yes, but what if someone *does* notice?" I say, worried and close to tears. "I want to keep on playing hockey."

"Abby, if we don't provide the certificate, you won't be allowed to play," Mom gently reminds me.

Even though I'm convinced that my season will end sooner than expected, I give up. I'm angry—with myself! If I were as ordinary as Scotty, no one would have noticed me and I would be able to play without the threat of my true identity being revealed to the world.

That will teach me!

In the end, it's agreed that my father will send a copy of my birth certificate to Mr. Grossi.

I cross my fingers and pray hard to the hockey gods that my certificate will go unnoticed.

Two days later, reality hits. The phone rings. I answer. My heart racing, I hand the receiver to my mother. "It's Mr. Grossi..."

"Have faith," whispers Mom before talking to the Tee Pees coach.

My brothers and father, who were playing table hockey in the living room, interrupt their game to join us.

"Actually, Mr. Grossi," says Mom after a few seconds, "it's not Mrs. Samuel Hoffman. I didn't take my husband's name. It's Mrs. Dorothy Medhurst, thank you." It's all said in a polite, but firm way.

People have called my mother eccentric. She's a former athlete, but mostly she's an artist. She has a job, she goes by her maiden name, she doesn't wear the latest fashion, she's different. We have no television at home but plenty of books. And she cares about other people. For instance, she pays our cleaning lady more than she herself earns in a day. Our neighbors don't really understand. Dorothy Medhurst is a woman of heart and mind. I admire her so much. I hope to be like her when I'm older.

My mother smiles. "No, Mr. Grossi. We didn't make a mistake. We didn't send you the birth certificate of Ab's sister. In fact, she doesn't have a sister, only brothers."

Mom just spilled the beans. She referred to me using the pronoun *she*. The dice are cast.

"Yes, *she*...Ab is short for Abby or Abigail. Are you still there, Mr. Grossi?" she asks.

She cups her hand over the receiver so he doesn't hear. "Either the shock has made him speechless, or he has fainted," she says with mischief in her eyes.

I don't find that funny.

"You would have heard the body hit the floor," remarks Dad. "He's probably just in shock."

"Yes, Mr. Grossi...What were you saying?"

"Good heavens, no! Who would name a boy Abigail? It's a girl's name because, Mr. Grossi, Abigail, Abby, or Ab, if you prefer, is a girl!"

"*WHAT?*" The voice at the other end of the line is so loud that everyone in the kitchen hears it. Little Benny imitates it: "What? What? What? What? What?"

Muni takes him to the living room. The conversation continues in a tone that doesn't please my mother. She moves the receiver away from her ear. I come closer so I can hear what Mr. Grossi is screaming.

"...three months later, you're telling me that Hoffman, my star defenseman, is in fact Abigail Hoffman, a girl?"

My mother is unfazed. It takes a lot more that this to ruffle her feathers. "Wasn't Abby selected for the all-star team because of her talent? Didn't she clearly show that she's capable of playing on the same rink as boys her—

"Don't interrupt me, Mr. Grossi!" Right now, my mother reminds me of a lioness who would do anything to protect her young. "What difference does it make, Mr. Grossi? Did Abby bother anyone? Be honest."

And then she bursts out laughing. It's the kind of laugh that lightens any situation, no matter how tense. In fact, we hear Al Grossi laugh too. I'm relieved. Slightly...

"We'll be there, Mr. Grossi. Have a good evening!" She hangs up.

"So, Dorothy Medhurst?" asks Dad. The fact that his wife didn't take his name is the least of his concerns.

Muni comes back to the kitchen with Little Benny on his shoulders. He wants to hear what happened.

"We've been asked to attend an emergency meeting with the authorities of the league on Friday night. They want to discuss Abby's case."

I try to understand the purpose of this meeting. "Does that mean I can play or not?"

My mother would rather tell me the truth than create false hope. "I don't know, Abby. It was a shock for these gentlemen to discover that a girl has made her way into an organization of four hundred boys of all ages. We upset the apple cart."

"But if they want to stop you from playing, they'll have to contend with your mother!" adds Dad. "And with us!"

"Yeah!" my brothers emphasize, sticking their chests out.

I'm only half reassured.

But that was before I found out that Phyllis Griffiths was on our side...

Chapter 14

Phyllis Griffiths...the name is familiar. My father, an avid newspaper reader, reminds me why.

"She writes for the Sports section of the *Toronto Telegram*."

We're in the car, on our way to Varsity Arena for a summit meeting with Mr. Grossi. Muni is with us, but Paul stayed home to watch Little Benny. Or to talk in peace with his Erica.

Phyllis Griffiths. Yes, that's it! I clipped some of her articles about Althea Gibson, the famous American tennis player. A black athlete, Gibson had to overcome prejudices and racism in order to become one of the greatest champions of her sport. She's an idol of mine.

Ms. Griffiths is one of the rare woman journalists at the *Telegram*. In the Sports department, her presence is almost as strange as an Abigail with the Tee Pees! Did she cut off her hair and sign Phil on the employment form when the newspaper hired her? The comparison makes me smile. However, I don't see how she could influence anyone.

"She wants to write your story in her paper. It will give weight to your case," says Mom, who, though they're not close friends, has known the journalist for several years.

My mother used to play elite basketball and Phyllis Griffiths refereed some of her games. Because of Phyllis's honesty, good judgment, and deep understanding of the game, my mother had the utmost respect for her. Respect for a referee? My mother has always been incredibly open-minded!

"Phyllis was a basketball player herself. She was one of the most talented athletes of her university," notes Mom.

Though the days are getting longer—a sign that spring is coming—it's dark when we arrive at Varsity Arena. We just had time to eat dinner before leaving for the meeting.

The meeting is in chairman Earl Graham's office, near the locker rooms. We hear the echo of pucks bouncing off the boards. The Junior Tee Pees are training for their game against Hamilton on Saturday.

At the other end of the hall leading to Graham's office, I see two men talking and smoking cigarettes. They throw us a mocking glance, and disappear into the office.

"The Welcome Committee," says Dad.

"Faceoff!" declares Mom, ready to take on whoever wants to fight her.

Behind us, a woman calls out, "Dorothy!"

My mother stops abruptly. Following close behind, Muni and I bump into her and almost knock her over but she manages to catch herself. When she discovers Phyllis Griffiths, her face lights up.

"You came!" she says, sounding relieved. The two women shake hands…like men! But no violent slaps on the shoulders mark this reunion.

Phyllis is an elegant woman in her early fifties, so a dozen years older than my mother. She's fairly tall, athletic-looking, with a square jaw and short graying hair. Her green eyes sparkle with youthful curiosity.

She turns toward me. "So you're the famous Abby Hoffman?"

Muni pulls my father's coat sleeve. "Isn't she supposed to be Ab Hoffman when we're at the arena?" he whispers.

"Not anymore, son," answers Dad. He checks his watch. "Let's not keep these gentlemen waiting."

Phyllis is warm and talks to me as if I'm an adult while we make our way to the chairman's office. "Would you like me to write about you in my newspaper, Abby?"

"Uh…I don't know…Yes…Why?"

She pulls a notebook and a pen from the pocket of her coat. "I'd like to tell your story to the entire country."

"Isn't Canada too big to pay attention to one small girl?" I asked, surprised.

A man with a serious face invites us in the chairman's office. As soon as I step into the small room I see Coach Grossi. I wave at him. He simply nods.

The atmosphere is icy and you can feel the tension. *All of this because of me?* My heart beats faster. I feel like I'm being called into the school principal's office because I've done something terrible.

Chairs have been arranged around a table. There aren't enough of them to seat everyone. Chairman Graham goes to my parents and politely introduces himself. In addition to him and Mr. Grossi, three men—all directors of the Little Toronto Hockey League—are present. Their severe attitude reminds me that hockey is serious business. But it's only a game!

When he hears Phyllis Griffiths' name, the chairman tenses up. "The *Telegram* reporter? What are you doing here?"

"My job, Mr. Graham," she answers, not at all intimidated.

"This is a private meeting, Ms. Griffiths," insists Al Grossi. "You're not allowed to attend."

"However, the right of a young girl to play hockey is of public interest, Sir," replies Phyllis. *Tit for tat.* In hockey terms, I would say this was a solid, legal bodycheck.

Chairman Graham invites people to sit around the table. The five men are smoking cigarette after cigarette so the place quickly fills with smoke. My eyes itch. My parents, who don't smoke, are uncomfortable too. So is Muni, who has asthma and is now coughing.

Muni, Phyllis, and I don't have chairs. None of these gentlemen is polite enough to offer his chair to the journalist.

"The kids and Ms. Griffiths will have to leave so we can talk freely," says one of the directors, the one with the thick black moustache hiding his upper lip. "Those of you who are not sitting are invited to step out of the room."

My parents exchange a look and, to our hosts' surprise, my father gives his chair to the journalist so she can sit next to my mother. "We'll be nearby," says Dad.

He takes leave of the directors: "Good luck, gentlemen," he says, deadpan.

He leads us out of the room and closes the door behind him. My father knows his Dorothy, and he has faith in her capacity to face this "tribunal."

I wish I could attend the meeting. I'm the one

concerned after all. "It's unfair," I say, sullen. This whole thing is biased."

"Yeah," adds Muni. "It's five men against two women…"

My father smiles. "It is unfair. Those poor men! They have no idea what they're in for!"

I could sit in the bleachers with Muni and watch the Junior Tee Pees. But the action is not in the rink; it's here, on the other side of that door. So I'd rather stay nearby. Voices are already rising. We listen closely and share what we hear.

"…a shame…a scandal!…"

A man…Probably a director…

"…what will people say?"

That's from the one with the moustache, I think. He's the type of person who worries about what other people think. He has no valid argument. He just scored in his own net.

"…and why wouldn't I write that?" Phyllis, the three of us agree.

Overlapping voices…Impossible to make out who is saying what…

"…expelled from the team…"

"What if we don't say anything?"

"That's ridiculous!"

"Ladies and gentlemen, let's stay calm!"

Al Grossi, I bet.

"One at a time…"

That's Chairman Graham, not very talkative up until now.

"…are furious because you've been had by a nine-year-old girl who just wanted to play hockey!"

Ah! That's my mother!

"She lied to us! She's discrediting the league…"

A director, one of the smokers…

We hear noises in the hall. The Junior Tee Pees are going back to their locker room. They have to walk by us. Muni and I, used to admiring them from the top of the bleachers, are impressed by their stature and their bulk.

Ab McDonald is the team's assistant captain. He has dark eyes, a little like Maurice Richard from the Montreal Canadiens. I wave at him timidly and say "Hi!"

He stops in front of me. On his skates, he's taller than my father, who is pretty tall.

"What are you doing here? Are you waiting for someone?" he asks, his face covered in sweat.

Muni explains with great energy the reason for our presence in the hall. I'm not sure it's a good idea, but it's too late.

McDonald looks from my brother to my father, then finally rests his eyes on me. I feel like a circus attraction. "Well, I'll be damned!" he eventually says. "What's your real name? Ab stands for…?"

"Abby…What about you?"

"In my case, it's a little more complicated. Ab stands for Alvin Brian!" he says with a laugh. "I can't believe it! A girl who plays hockey!"

I fire back. "I'm allowed!" I don't care that he's an assistant captain; he can't tell me that a girl shouldn't play hockey. McDonald realizes that he went too far.

"Yes, you're right, Abby. Why shouldn't you play?"

Reassured, I tell him that I wear the number 6, like him; that I play defense, like him; that my team is called the Tee Pees, like his; but that unlike him, I'm not an assistant captain.

"I'm sure you're very good."

"She's been selected for the Little Toronto Hockey League All-Star Team," says Dad. "That's why we're here. So she can get permission to keep playing."

Ab McDonald points to the office door with his glove. "Is there a man with a thick black moustache in there?"

"Yes. And he's downright ugly!" spits Muni.

"He's a family friend," says Ab, a weird expression on his face.

Big mistake, Muni!

Maybe Ab could have been an ally. Now we probably lost him because of Muni.

"Can't you ever keep your mouth shut?" I lash out at my brother.

"Sorry, McD," stutters Muni, adding insult to injury.

"McD?" repeats Ab McDonald.

"Yes, that's what we call you in the bleachers: McD…"

The player's expression lightens. He was just playing with us! "It's true that his moustache is horrible. It looks like an old broom!"

McDonald removes his glove and knocks on the door. He positions me in front of him. Then, without waiting for an invitation, we enter. Anyone else interrupting that meeting would have been sent packing. That is abundantly clear from the expressions on the men's faces. However, those expressions turn to admiration and respect when they discover, standing behind me, the identity of the person who dared to disturb them.

Being assistant captain of the city's junior team comes with its privileges.

"Oh, Ab!" exclaims the man with the moustache.

"Our brave assistant captain," adds another director.

Ab McDonald ignores them and chooses to greet the journalist instead. "Good evening, Ms. Griffiths. It's always a pleasure to see you."

"Same here, my dear Alvin Brian," she replies with a nod. "Do you know Dorothy Medhurst? She's Abby Hoffman's mom."

Ab McDonald goes to my mother and shakes her hand. "I could have sworn you were her big sister," he says. The assistant captain is slathering it on a little thick.

"We're in the middle of an extraordinary meeting," indicates chairman Earl Graham, almost as an apology.

The player moves toward the exit. He puts a hand on my shoulder. "I just wanted to say how wonderful it is that my friend—he stresses the word—Abby here is allowed to play hockey with boys."

Suddenly, the men's hostility seems to give way to resignation.

"You're showing great wisdom and open-mindedness, ladies and gentlemen. After all, we're about to enter the Sixties, aren't we?" Ab says.

"I...I guess," the man with the moustache feels obliged to respond.

Before leaving, McDonald extends an invitation to me in a loud voice to make sure everyone can hear. "Abby, would you like to skate with us during one of our pregame warm-ups?"

I don't hesitate for a second. "Of course!" I jump up and down in excitement.

"Let me organize it," he says. "People should know that girls are capable of playing hockey!"

The message was intended more for the directors than for me.

As he closes the door, he winks at me. "It's up to you now, Abby!"

Chapter 15

Did Ab McDonald have a real influence in my case? My mother thinks he did. On the drive home after the meeting, she tells us that after the assistant captain stepped in, the wind turned in my favor.

McDonald's family friend—the man with the moustache—became less blunt, as if McDonald had shaken his convictions.

Phyllis Griffiths took notes throughout the entire meeting. This irritated and even intimidated the directors. The presence of the *Telegram* journalist also contributed to the favorable outcome.

I'm curious to know what Al Grossi said about me. My mother doesn't answer; she remains vague about my coach's feelings. "He and the chairman were standing to the side. I was under the impression they were reflecting on the consequences of this decision."

"The consequences?" I say, perplexed.

"What will happen next, if you prefer," says Mom.

Indeed, how could they justify forbidding a young girl to practice her favorite sport? Or how could they explain the fact that this same young girl fooled everyone for three months?

We are standing in a group outside the room because the directors asked my mother and Ms. Griffiths to leave so they could come to a decision.

After ten long minutes, they opened the door and invited us in for the announcement of the verdict. I was watching Mr. Grossi, eyes glued to the floor, arms folded over his chest. I was convinced that my season was over.

With calculated slowness, Phyllis wet the end of her pencil with her tongue. She then rested it on her notebook, ready to record the decision. I saw in her eyes that she wouldn't spare any of these men if they stopped me from playing with the Tee Pees.

Chairman Graham addressed us in a pompous and solemn tone, the kind of tone used for official announcements.

"We, the directors of the Little Toronto Hockey League, have agreed, following a split vote, that Abby Hoffman will no longer be able to…"

He let the end of the sentence trail off. *That's so cruel!* I lowered my head. My fabulous season had just ended in a dusty office of Varsity Arena. I could hardly hold back my tears.

"...will no longer be able to change in the Tee Pees locker room. She'll have to change in my office so as not to arouse the boys or be aroused herself."

He looked at me with a thin smile, as did Al Grossi. *What?* Did I hear this right?

My mother congratulated the directors but without shaking their hands. I had a feeling she wanted to keep her distance.

"Gentlemen," she said in a similar tone, "I applaud your decision and I thank you for it. However, I still don't understand why the fact that a girl plays hockey with boys was cause enough for a summit meeting."

"It's never happened before, Mrs. Hoffman," said Earl Graham, trying to make excuses for himself.

"It's Ms. Medhurst," Mom corrected. She's a stickler when it comes to her name.

Irritated, one of the directors whispered: "Now we know who the girl takes after..."

I heard him. "Yes, and I'm proud of it, Sir," I said, staring into his eyes.

Before leaving, my mother asked for a written document confirming their judgment. "In case you change your minds," she explained.

"That won't be necessary, Dorothy. I have it all down," indicated Phyllis Griffiths, tapping her notebook with her pencil.

Just as I was walking out, Coach Grossi called me. "I'll see you at the game tomorrow night, Ab," he said, extending his hand.

I was relieved he wasn't ignoring me anymore. His words confirmed my status as a hockey player more than any signed document ever would.

Phyllis Griffiths spends Saturday afternoon with the Hoffmans. She asks me all kinds of questions that have nothing to do with hockey.

"Who do you think is going to be interested in this story?" I ask her.

She smiles. "More people than you think, Abigail."

"Call me Ab or Abby, okay?"

Sitting at the kitchen table, I tell her how I registered for the Little Toronto Hockey League. My father adds some more details.

"Someone had told me that girls were not allowed to play. Meanwhile, Abby figured out a way to register at a different table. The first thing I knew, she was on the ice, skating with the boys! She came to us to announce that she had been registered."

While we're talking, two-year-old Little Benny

is playing in the living room with a stick and puck. He shoots the puck against one of several cardboard boxes that act as boards. All the boxes are filled with sports equipment except one, which contains stones that Paul and his friend have collected at Silver Crater Mine; they're both members of The Walker Mineralogical Club in Toronto.

"The older kids are not allowed to use a puck," says Mom. "My concession was a rubber ball. Otherwise, the furniture and the walls would be completely destroyed."

"Yeah," says Muni, resigned. "There's only enough room to practice handling the stick. If it weren't for the piano, it'd be perfect."

I fire back. "What are you talking about? Even with the piano, it's perfect!"

My mother tells the journalist that I play regularly. "Abby just passed her Grade 4 piano exam, with *Minuet in D Minor* by Johann Sebastian Bach, one of her best pieces. Would you like to hear it, Phyllis?"

"Nooooo!" plead my brothers. "She plays it all day long!"

Our guest is polite. "Yes, I'd love to hear it, if you don't mind, Abby…"

"We mind," retort Paul and Muni.

I go to the piano. "Stop whining," I tell my brothers. "The piece doesn't even last a minute."

"It feels like a century every time," objects Paul. But I

suspect he appreciates my piano playing.

My performance over, I bow to my audience. Everyone claps but not for the same reasons: Phyllis and my parents because they liked it; Paul and Muni because it's over.

"You play piano like you would a typewriter," teases Muni, imitating my teacher's nasal voice.

"If we could rig the piano so it doesn't make sound, that'd be fine with us," adds Paul.

"It wouldn't stop me from practicing!" I tell them before going back to my chair.

"Abby also does drama," says Mom. "She acted in a Christmas play at school."

"It was a tragedy," remembers Paul, making a face.

"A drama," adds Muni.

"I was the servant of the three wise men," I tell Phyllis, paying no attention to my brothers.

Little Benny shoots the puck and scores—on Phyllis's shin.

"A future Maple Leafs player," she says, gritting her teeth and rubbing her leg.

Little Benny apologizes and goes back to playing with Paul and Muni.

"Are your brothers hockey players, Abby?"

"Yes, Paul is the goalie for Humberside Collegiate. He had a shutout against Danforth yesterday, and his team won the championship."

I tell Phyllis that my older brother didn't intend to start the season with that team because he felt he wasn't good enough. But Trevor Kaye, a Humberside player, saw Paul play at the rink near our house and suggested he join his team. Coach Bill Rowland put Paul in the net in the fourth game and Humberside never lost again!

"I also play for Harringtons in the Ki-Y league!" yells Paul from the living room.

"And I scored thirty-eight goals in my season," adds Muni from the same place. "I'm the team captain and Muni is spelled with an 'i' not a 'y.'"

"It's spelled like the American actor Paul Muni," notes Mom.

"Ah, I see! Paul and Muni. That's fun," says Phyllis.

My father explains that Muni is center for the Concords in the Atom League, and also plays for Annette Street Public School juniors.

"And you, Samuel?" asks Phyllis.

"Oh, I don't play hockey!" he laughs. I'm a chemist at Canadian Industries Limited."

The journalist notices the two bulletin boards on the wall—one for newspaper clippings about hockey, the other for the family schedule.

"It's the only way we can keep track of who is doing what during the week," explains Mom, who put that system in place last year.

Phyllis takes a closer look and thanks us when she

discovers some of her articles. She pauses in front of a booklet of tickets that is also tacked up on the board.

"Part of the money raised from selling those tickets will allow the league to continue its activities next year," explains Dad.

"So far, I've sold twenty-four books of ten tickets. Would you like to buy one?" I ask Phyllis.

"Abby!" scolds Mom.

The journalist doesn't take offense at my enthusiastic sales technique. She buys a booklet for a dollar.

"You work hard for your league, Abby," she says, handing me a brand new one-dollar bill.

I smile, embarrassed. "Well…to be honest, I'm working hard for myself! There are prizes for the best sellers, like hockey pants, gloves, a stick, a puck—" I run to my bedroom and come right back to show her my hockey stockings. "I wish they were giving away stockings too."

I can slip my fingers through the gaping holes, including the one at the knee.

"No skates among the prizes?" wonders Phyllis.

"No, those are too expensive! Right now, I have the ones Paul and then Muni used to wear. I hope to get a new pair. Little Benny will inherit mine. I'll also need shoulder pads if I play next year. And I'd love to ski and—"

"Abby, you're making Phyllis dizzy," says Mom.

"I'm told you're also a good swimmer," says the

journalist while looking at her notes.

"Yes, I swim at the Lakeshore Club. But I stopped this winter because I love hockey the very best!"

Paul and Muni abandon their activities and come back to the table.

"Abby is very fast at breast stroke and on her back. She's a little fish," remarks Dad.

"I've never seen a fish swim on its back," says Muni.

"Actually, when it's on its back, it doesn't swim any more at all," adds Paul.

"And what do you want to do in life? You, Paul…"

"A solitary geologist."

"Muni?"

"Me? A garbage collector with a bunch of kids."

"And you, Abby?"

"No kids for me! I want to be a school teacher, or a gold prospector so I can make a fortune."

Little Benny taps Phyllis on the knee.

"I want to be a cloud."

My mother interrupts us, indicating the clock. "Abby, you have a game tonight."

What a strange situation!

With Phyllis Griffiths and my parents at my side, I rush past the Tee Pees locker room at Varsity Arena, hoping they won't see me.

"Hey! Ab! Where are you going?"

I recognize the voice of David Kurtis. He approaches, his skates slung around his neck. "The locker room is here," he reminds me, intrigued by my absent-minded attitude.

"I know but I have to…go over there first. I'll see you later." I turn around to put an end to our conversation.

"What's wrong with Ab?" David asks Phyllis.

The journalist thinks for a moment. "Are you coming, Ms. Griffiths?" I say while keeping at a safe distance.

"Yes, I'll be right there, Abby," she answers.

"Abby?" repeats David, looking confused. "That's not a boy's name…"

"You're right, young man," declares Phyllis in a serious voice. "Abby is a girl's name—and your teammate is a girl named Abby."

David doesn't react right away. As I move closer to pull Phyllis out of there, he bursts out laughing.

"Ha! Ha! Ha! That's very funny! You almost fooled me. Ab is a girl…"

"Yes, very funny," I say, forcing a smile.

David disappears into the locker room to share the joke with the others.

"They'll have to hear about it sooner or later, right?" says Phyllis.

In a way, this "joke" broke the ice in the locker room, where I go once I have put on all my equipment.

Chapter 16

As soon as I show up at his office door, Mr. Graham greets me and leaves the room, as if he were afraid of being seen with me.

Notebook and pencil in hand, Phyllis asks his opinion about the eventual creation of a hockey league for girls, organized by the Little Toronto Hockey League. My parents brought up that possibility earlier, when we were on our way to the arena.

"It's not a bad idea," Mr. Graham answers cautiously, "if there are others like Abby, of course."

I leave them to their conversation and go into the office. Mr. Graham has cleared a corner for me and brought in a coat hanger for my jacket, and a chair so I can sit and tie my skates. Very thoughtful of him.

Phyllis knocks on the door and enters. Not at all intimidated, she sits behind the desk, in the chairman's chair.

"Make yourself at home," says Mr. Graham with sarcasm.

"Comfortable chair, Chairman," she says."The man understands that his office is not his anymore.

"Shall I close the door while Abby puts on her equipment?" he asks.

"Why? I only have to put on my skates," I say. "You know what? I'm the only hockey player, even among professionals, with a private changing room."

Phyllis is amused, but Mr. Graham mumbles a vague excuse and steps out.

"It's too bad," I say more seriously. "I would much rather be in the locker room with the guys. Why does it matter that I'm a girl? I feel like a stranger with my own team."

Phyllis looks over her notes. "Some of the people who will read the article will argue that girls should wear dresses, not hockey pants."

I pout. "Dresses are stupid! I'm lucky I go to a school where they let the girls wear jeans." My only dress is my Brownie uniform, which I'm forced to wear to go to church or to the restaurant with my Hoffman grandparents. "I'd rather talk hockey than fashion!" I say as I finish tying my skates.

Our conversation moves to another subject. "Okay. What's your favorite team, Abby? The Maple Leafs?"

"No, the Detroit Red Wings. They're the best."

"Any particular player?"

"No. We don't have a television at home. I've never seen a Leafs or a Red Wings game. That's just how it is."

Someone knocks on the door. It's Coach Grossi.

"Are you coming, Ab—" he hesitates "—*bee*? I'm going to talk to the team."

"I'd like to attend the meeting, if you don't mind," says Phyllis.

Al Grossi shrugs. "Sure, what's one more girl?" he replies, deadpan.

We head to the Tee Pees locker room. My teammates are surprised to see me already dressed. And all the more so when they recognize the journalist who seems to be following my every move.

I go to my usual place, between Scotty Hynek and David Kurtis, in silence.

"Why did you change somewhere else, Hoffman?" asks Scotty. "Another privilege?"

"It's not a privilege!"

Will the coach reveal my secret right away? Not with me here, I hope.

But Scotty is mainly concerned with Phyllis's

presence. "I thought the locker room was forbidden to women," he gripes. "We're being invaded!"

Then, after a hesitation, he exclaims, "Hey! I recognize her. She's Phyllis Griffiths, the *Toronto Telegram* sports writer! Is she here to meet me?"

Phyllis, who heard her name, waves at Scotty.

"See, Hoffman? She waved at me," he says, excited.

"She's not here for you, Scotty," declares David Kurtis, "she's here for Ab. She was talking with him earlier."

"Hoffman! What did he do to deserve this kind of attention? Did he learn to skate all of a sudden?"

"You'll understand soon...maybe," I tell him. Captain Jim Halliday is staring at me. Does he know? Was he warned about my situation because of his status? What I feel in his stare is not hostility, but curiosity. Then suddenly, as if he's made a decision, he nods in my direction and turns his attention back to the coach.

"Let me remind you that tonight, we're playing the Toronto Marlboros, the league leaders. If we win, we have a chance to make up ground and secure second place. If we lose, our opponents will be champions."

Mr. Grossi pauses to let his words sink in. And I suspect he's trying to give the journalist time to take notes because he just glanced at her. But Phyllis's arms remain crossed over her chest. If he's disappointed, the coach shows no sign of it.

No player in this locker room intends to slack off at this stage of the season. Each and every one of us loves to play hockey, whether at Varsity Arena or at an outdoor rink. The pleasure of skating, of running after a puck, of deking out a goalie, is like nothing else.

"I want to score my first goal," says Scotty, determined. "That really matters to me."

"I also have to talk to you about something else," adds Al Grossi, throwing a quick glance at Phyllis Griffiths.

Here we go! The time has come... I see Phyllis pull a pencil and notebook from her coat pocket. *How will the players react?* I inhale deeply to try to calm myself, but it doesn't work.

"As you all know," the coach begins, "there will be an all-star game on March 23rd."

I was wrong. Coach Grossi continues: "Four members of the Tee Pees have been selected for this game. I invite them to come to the center of the room when they hear their names—Jim Halliday, Russell Turnbull, David Kurtis and...Ab Hoffman."

"What about me?" asks Scotty. No one's paying attention to him.

The coach slaps the players on the butt to congratulate them. When he gets to me, he taps me lightly on the shoulder.

The Tee Pees cheer us by banging their sticks on the floor.

The coach gives each of us a pen and asks us to fill out a Player's Certificate. I write down the number on my jersey, as well as my address on Glendonwynne Road.

The certificate confirms my participation in the Timmy Tyke Tournament of March 23rd. It specifies that I'm a member of the Little Toronto Hockey League All-Star Team. The goal of the this game is explained in one sentence: "Boys on skates may help children who can't walk…" *Boys*…

"All proceeds from the game will go to the Ontario Society for Crippled Children," says the coach. An image pops into my mind: the smiling boy sitting in a wheelchair at the hospital.

I write my name at the bottom of the certificate, below Al Grossi's signature: Ab Hoffman, March, 3, 1956. Ab, not Abby, for luck. Chairman Earl Graham's signature is still missing. I hand the certificate back to the coach.

"Here you go, Sir."

"Thank you. Congratulations to you all," he applauds. Go back to your seats."

Just as I'm going to sit down, break away from the group, he pulls me by the sleeve. "You should get out on the ice, Abby," he suggests in a calm voice.

I heard him correctly. He said Abby, not Ab…

"The rest of us will catch up with you," Jim Halliday whispers to me.

So, to everybody's surprise, I slip out of the room. When I walk past Phyllis, she gives me a reassuring smile. "I'll see you in a bit," she tells me, knowingly.

Al Grossi closes the door behind me.

Our opponents, the Toronto Marlboros, are already on the ice. The players are skating and shooting at the goalie. In the other half of the rink—it must look very strange to the spectators—there's only one Tee Pees player. And she's a girl!

I have half of the surface to myself! I try to appreciate the moment and not worry too much about what's happening in the locker room. On the other hand, imagining Scotty's expression when he hears the truth makes me smile…"*What?*" he'll cry out, horrified. "All year, I got undressed next to a *girl?*" Then he'll faint…too funny!

I kill the time hitting wrist and backhand shots against the boards. I shoot from the blue line; when I miss, I retrieve the puck and immediately go back to my position. But I skate uneasily—I feel like I have lead in my skates.

From the corner of my eye, I notice that Phyllis is now standing near our bench. She's furiously scribbling in her notebook. What was said in that locker room?

My teammates appear behind her. I try to ignore them and act as if everything is normal. Which is what they do too. They get into their normal routine, going through pre-game warm up.

Sometimes I feel them staring at me, but whenever I make eye contact, they look away. Finally, David Kurtis, who's waiting for his turn to shoot at Graham Powell, grabs my arm and whispers in my ear: "Is it true, Ab? Is it true that you're a girl?"

"Yes. Is there a problem with that?" I say in a detached tone while I continue to handle the puck.

David lets out a nervous laugh. "No, because you play like a boy anyway."

Scotty has his back to me. "Did you leave your doll at home, Abigail?" he teases, in a low voice.

If there's one boy on this team whose opinion I couldn't care less about, it's Scotty Hynek. Jim Halliday shields me from Scotty with his body.

"Uh…Ab…You're one of the gang. We don't want to lose you. You're a good hockey player." He taps my pads with his stick.

Phew! I feel like a huge weight has been lifted from my shoulders. Suddenly I skate with much more ease. Russell Turnbull approaches with a big grin.

"I sure was fooled, Ab! Gee, I don't know what to say. But we want you to stay on the team. And you should put on your skates in the locker room with us. We won't look at you! Since you've been gone, Scotty has become unbearable. I think he misses you!"

"Liar!" Scotty replies.

The referee blows his whistle to start the game. On the ice, representing the Tee Pees, is Jim Halliday's offensive line and David Kurtis and I as defensemen.

From my position at the blue line, I hear the two referees at center ice speak with Jim.

"We heard there's a girl on your team, Halliday. Is that true?" asks Bob Hull.

"Maybe," Jim answers casually. "Who told you?"

"Our assistant captain, Ab McDonald," answers Hull.

McDonald and Hull play for the Junior Tee Pees. They make a little money on the side by working as referees for young kids' games.

"You want to know who it is?" says Halliday, "then find out for yourself!"

"Good idea!" Hull agrees, juggling the puck. "Beauchamp, you want to bet?"

"I'm in," says his fellow referee. "We try to identify the girl before the end of the game. We tell you our pick. The loser will have to referee for a week and give his pay to the winner."

"Deal!" declares Bob Hull.

"What?" interjects a player from the Marlboros. "We're playing against girls?"

"Against one girl," Jim Halliday specifies. "A single girl. And a lot of boys!"

Before we even face off, the rumor has spread like

wildfire—on the ice, on the players' bench, and all the way into the bleachers.

In the first minute of the game, I find myself fighting a Marlie in the corner of my zone. I knock him hard against the boards, grab the puck and pass it to Russell Turnbull, who completely misses it. I notice the Tee Pees are watching me skate as if it were the first time…This is insane!

During a break, Coach Grossi gathers his team to address the problem. "Where are your heads?" he explodes. "Concentrate on the game and forget everything else."

His outburst has the intended result. The Tee Pees crank up their efforts and forget that the defenseman with jersey number 6 is a girl. For me, it doesn't make much of a difference.

We can't say the same about the two referees. Busy trying to identify "the girl" among the Tee Pees, they make mistake after mistake and miss obvious offsides, one of which leads to a goal by the Marlboros.

Al Grossi is furious. He grabs Scotty's glasses—Scotty is on the bench—and waves them at the referees. "You need them more than he does!"

Scotty is stunned by the coach's behavior. He rolls his eyes, irritated. When he turns to the coach again, one of his eyes—the right one—is still staring at the ceiling! I mention it to him.

"My glasses!" says Scotty, his hand extended.

The coach, who changes color as quickly as he loses his temper, apologizes and returns the glasses. Scotty immediately heads for the locker room. When he returns a few seconds later, his eyes are back to normal.

"No questions, Miss Hoffman!" he hisses.

The game progresses at a good pace. I try to play normally, without overdoing it to prove what a girl is capable of. I've already proven that during the entire season.

When the siren goes off at the end of the game, we crowd around our goalie, happy with a 4-2 win over the Marlboros.

Referees Hull and Beauchamp join us, their eyes sparkling. "Wait! Don't leave yet!" warns Bobby Hull.

"Yes! We know who the girl is," adds Referee Beauchamp.

Rather than going back to their locker room, the Toronto Marlboros move in closer. They, too, want to know who the girl is. Their petty comments swirl around me.

"She's the one who can't skate…"

"She's the one who can't shoot…" (That one, I take note of: number 14. Next time he's going to kiss the boards.)

"She's the one who cries if you touch her…"

"She's the one who brought her doll…"

Referee Hull blows his whistle to shut them up.

"You're worse than a bunch of girls talking on the phone!"

He points a finger in my direction. "It's her!"

That's it…I've been discovered.

"Me?"

Behind me, Scotty bursts into a nasty laugh.

"It's so obvious, Hoffman!"

But Referee Hull and his colleague correct me.

"No, not you, Hoffman. Her…behind you."

"Yes," adds Beauchamp, "the girl with the glasses…"

"Who? *Me?*" exclaims Scotty.

Chapter 17

"It's too much, isn't it?" I ask the members of my family, all leaning over the kitchen table. "I just want to play hockey, not make the headlines like the Toronto Maple Leafs!"

"No," answers Mom, moved. "You deserve it."

She read Phyllis Griffiths's article in the Thursday, March 8, 1956 edition of the *Toronto Telegram*. My father and my brothers are nodding in agreement. Soft light from the ceiling lamp falls on the newspaper, open to the Sports section.

It's not the Red Wings' loss 6-4 to the Montreal Canadiens last night that holds our attention. And it's not the short article about the Maple Leafs' battle for a place in the Stanley Cup playoffs. (They're trying hard to defeat the Boston Bruins. A photo of George Armstrong accompanies the article.) Nor is it the article about Toronto playing the powerful Canadiens tonight at Maple Leaf Gardens.

What monopolizes our attention is a headline, written in big black letters: "ROUGH, HARDCHECKING AB BACK ON THE ICE—SHE IS." Then, in smaller type, the byline: by Phyllis Griffiths, *Telegram* Staff Reporter.

The article is long, very long...too long for my taste. How did Phyllis include in a single article everything she saw and heard at home and at Varsity Arena last Saturday? With the photograph, the article almost fills an entire page. Just for me.

The journalist tells my story in all its minute details, from my first time putting on skates when I was three, to my registration with the Little Toronto Hockey League in the fall of 1955.

She writes about my taste in clothing (or, when it comes to dresses, my distaste in clothing), my favorite subjects at school (geography, arithmetic, spelling—it's funny, I don't remember telling her that), my piano lessons, and the Detroit Red Wings.

She even includes information about my parents and my brothers. (She spelled Muni without a "y." Too bad, I would have loved to tease him about that.)

Oh! Here's something funny! She asked a few Tee

Pees players about their reaction when they discovered there was a girl on the team. David Kurtis thought that Phyllis was joking. He came back ten minutes later, clutched her arm, and asked if it were true that Ab was a girl!

I was touched when I read that Captain Jim Halliday more or less repeated what he told me at the rink: "He—she—is just one of the gang. I hope we won't lose him—her, I mean."

Same thing for super scorer Russell Turnbull, star center on the first line. "I was fooled, like everyone else. But we want to keep Ab on our team, there's no doubt about that!"

Referees Hull and Beauchamp's reaction also made me smile. Especially since they couldn't identify the girl and mistakenly pointed at Scotty at the end of the game.

"Number 6 was just another hockey player to me," declared Beauchamp.

And according to Coach Grossi, Ab is "one of the best players on the team. His bodychecks are powerful." But he admits being flabbergasted when he learned, before everyone else, that Ab's real name was Abigail…

Finally, Phyllis mentions two important games coming up at Varsity Arena in March: the annual Jamboree on Friday 16th to raise funds for the league's future activities, and the all-star game on Friday 23rd to benefit disabled kids.

Yes, a lot of details. And it's all the more embarrassing because since all five of us can't read the article at the same time, my mother is reading it out loud.

And then there's the photo. A shot of me from head to skates, leaning on my stick. You can clearly see my name on the stick: Ab Hoffman. Luckily, the hole in my stocking on the right knee is not too visible.

The photo was taken by the *Telegram* photographer assisting Phyllis after Saturday night's meet against the Marlboros. He made me skate slowly toward him. He didn't want a classic pose, like for a face off. I had to do it over again several times and so did he. It was awkward because during the short photo shoot, which felt like an hour to me, none of the Tee Pees or Marlie players left the rink.

To make things worse, Scotty Hynek kept harassing the photographer. "I'm the girl! I'm the girl! Not him! Hoffman is a boy!"

My proud father goes to the board—the one with the newspaper clippings. He takes all the clippings down. My mother hands him Phyllis's article and he pins it on the board.

Little Benny is awake and shows up, all grumbly. He's rubbing his eyes, blinded by the kitchen light. He cuddles in my arms. He's still numb with sleep.

When he sees my photo, he jolts awake and shouts, "Abby! Abby!"

The phone rings. My parents exchange a worried glance. When the phone rings this early in the morning, it's never good news. My father picks up. After a few seconds, he relaxes and smiles at me.

"Yes, after school," he says into the receiver. "At Varsity Arena. Abby will be there with her equipment. Thank you, Sir. Good-bye."

"That was someone from the Canadian Broadcasting Corporation. They read Phyllis's article and the TV producers want to meet you tonight," he explains.

I shrug. "We don't even have a TV."

"We'll go to grandpa Albert's place," says Paul.

"Do the CBC people also want to meet Abby Hoffman's big brothers?" asks Muni.

My father shakes his head. "Not this time, guys. Sorry."

The phone rings again. My mother answers this time.

"Yes, thank you, Divine…Uh…Mrs. Hoffman. I will give her the message."

My Hoffman grandparents want to congratulate me on the *Telegram* article. My mother barely has time to hang up, and me to appreciate their call before the phone rings again.

My father picks up. His smile disappears in a flash. His cheeks turn red, his expression becomes hard. I've never seen him like this. He moves the receiver away from his ear. It's a man's voice. I catch a few words.

...figure skating...dress...shame...tomboy...

My father pulls himself together. "Sir," he says, trying to stay calm. "I had no idea cavemen could read newspapers and use telephones. Good-bye!"

He hangs up. "How rude!"

I'm upset. "What did I do to him?"

"Abby," Mom says gently, "there are people in this world who can't cope with change. Don't pay attention to them."

I'm flabbergasted. "All I want is to play hockey."

My mother suggests I get ready for school. From my room, I hear the phone ring repeatedly. In the time it takes me to get dressed and brush my teeth, two more requests for newspaper and radio interviews have come in.

●

Few kids from school have read the *Telegram* article. But many saw the photograph. All of a sudden, the schoolyard becomes too small.

As soon as I step on the school grounds, I'm surrounded by a mob of students. Most of them congratulate me, some ask for an autograph. Boys older than me take pleasure in mocking me.

I don't talk to anyone because all the voices register as a single block of sound. It's making me dizzy. I don't recognize anyone anymore. Yes, I do recognize one voice—Susie Read's.

"Hey, Abby! Come over here!" I feel a hand pull my coat sleeve and extract me from the crowd. Some kids object.

"Hey! She's not yours! Abby belongs to everyone now." Susie ignores them and drags me away.

"All of this because I'm a girl who plays hockey with boys," I say, shaken.

"Forget about it. In two days, no one will remember. Hockey is not that important."

Stung by her comment, I fire back, "Well, it's more important than figure skating, Miss Ann Barbara Scott!"

"You don't even know what you're talking about," Susie flares up. "For one thing, it's *Barbara Ann* Scott.[1] Hockey is turning you into a real tomboy, Mr. Armstrong George!"

We look at each other and burst out laughing. My friend knows nothing about hockey. She knows the name of this Leafs player because George Armstrong is her father's favorite. The bell calls us to class. Susie and I run toward the school, but once again I'm slowed down by kids who want to meet me, touch me, question me, encourage me, criticize me. There's something for every taste:

---

[1] Canadian figure skater: Canadian, European, World Champion 1944-48; Olympic gold medalist 1948

"Do you shower with the guys?" (a girl's voice)

"Do you wear a jock?" (a boy's voice)

One comment delights me: "You're my favorite player!"

A first-grader is standing in front of me, all bundled up in winter clothes, face hidden under a tuque pulled way down, and a scarf covering the nose. I can't tell whether it's an Ab or an Abby. There's only one way to find out:

"What's your name?"

"Me?" says the kid, thrilled that someone is taking an interest in him or her. "It's Alex."

This creates a chain reaction. All the kids want me to know their names. It gives me a headache!

Ms. Morley, rescues me. She lets me into the school before everyone else "You've become a real star, Abigail!" she says to tease me.

I hang my coat in the hall near my classroom and take off my boots. Once I get to my desk, she hands me a blank piece of paper.

"May I have your autograph? It's for my daughter, Nellie. I read the newspaper article to her this morning. She was very impressed, as I was. She loves hockey."

●

The situation doesn't improve much over the next few hours. Apparently, all the teachers brought the *Telegram* to school and read the article to their students. And they all made a point of telling them that the Abby Hoffman in question attends this school and is in third grade.

I have to make a presentation—completely improvised—to my class about my hockey season, which I have kept hidden from everyone up until now. It's like a punishment!

I spend my rare free time—the two recesses—surrounded by autograph hunters. I write on little pieces of paper, in notebooks and books, even on arms. At first, I sign my full name. Then, given the high number of requests, I cut it down to just my first name, Abigail, then to Abby, and finally to Ab.

Susie, who is not at all jealous of this sudden—and in my opinion, exaggerated—popularity is a privileged and amused witness. "You're a real George Armstrong, Abby Hoffman," she teases.

What I'm experiencing today, on a smaller scale, is probably what professional hockey players deal with every day. The price of glory.

And all of this because I play a boys' sport?

It's complete nonsense!

Chapter 18

The school secretary arrives to tell Ms. Morley that I am to report to the office of Mr. Williams, the principal, right away. She asks me to follow her.

I'm confused. Students called into the office usually have behaved badly or are having difficulties in class. I don't fall into either of these categories. Or at least, that's what I think.

My fears dissolve when Mr. Williams opens the door to his office with a smile. He invites me to sit and points to a stash of little pink papers. "These are all requests for interviews that I have received for you," he explains.

He shows me one of the papers. He's impressed and excited at the same time. "This one is from *The New York*

Times! Our Abby Hoffman is going to be in *The New York Times!*"

"Oh," I say. *The New York Times* means nothing to me.

Mr. Williams tells me that my mother will pick me up after school to go to the arena. She'll also bring my equipment. "And you have an interview with Ben Rose from the *Toronto Daily Star* before your interview with CBC Television."

He hands me the wad of little pink papers, which marks the end of our meeting. I read a few on my way back to class: the *Calgary Herald*, *La Presse* in Montreal… Oh! Phyllis Griffiths called…

Once again, the Hoffmans are on their way to Varsity Arena. My brothers are not letting me breathe for a second. "Abby, an autograph!" implores Paul. "I'm going to sell it at an auction and become a millionaire."

"Hey! She should be asking us for autographs," says Muni. "We're her idols. It says so in the newspaper!"

I protest: "I never said that…the reporter made a mistake!"

My mother doesn't like to take sides, but she steps in. "Phyllis is very professional, Abby. She's not known for making stuff up."

"Yeah, Abby!" teases Muni. "Even though you make stuff up!"

"Oh, stop bothering me!"

"Guys," warns Mom, "leave your sister alone. She has a big night ahead of her."

My father is in his lab, working overtime. He will catch up with us later. My mother packed food for us. We don't have time to go to a restaurant on a weeknight. But she doesn't want me to starve between interviews.

At Varsity Arena, Coach Grossi takes me under his wing. He informs me that the *Toronto Daily Star* is waiting for me in the locker room to shoot a series of photographs. Classical music coming from the rink indicates that it's figure skating time. Susie must be there. Thursday afternoon is when she practices for her end-of-the-year show.

Chairman Graham welcomes me and introduces me to journalist Ben Rose. Rose is shorter than my mother, and also younger. When he smiles, he has dimples in his cheeks. He seems nice.

"First the photographs, and then the interview," he says. He talks to the photographer and passes on his instructions.

"We'd like to shoot you while you tie your skates, like for a regular game."

Without any hesitation, I look at Chairman Graham and reply, "Well for a regular game, I wouldn't be allowed to change here with the other players."

All truth is good, I guess, but not all truth is good

to say. The chairman's eyes widen. He clears his throat. Finally, he steps out of the room. My mother gives me a knowing smile.

While I put on my skates, my little brother Benny grabs my stick and plays with a puck lying on the floor. The photographer takes a shot of me wearing my team jersey. I search through my hockey bag. "Mom, the Tee Pees jersey is not here," I say, disappointed.

"I had to wash it," she apologizes. "Little Benny put it on to play at being Abby Hoffman and he kept it on to eat. He dropped mustard on one of the sleeves."

My brother shoots the puck under a bench. "Scooores!" he screams. But he's so little he can't lift the stick in the air to celebrate his accomplishment. How could I be mad at him for mucking up my jersey?

"Never mind. What's important is you, Abby, not your jersey," Ben Rose reminds me.

My mother did bring the Canadiens jersey—the one that belonged to Paul first, then to Muni, and that will one day belong to Little Benny. That's the one I wear when I play in the outdoor rink at home.

"The Canadiens," notes the journalist. "Is that your favorite team?"

"No, my team is the Detroit Red Wings."

Once the photo is taken, Ben Rose sits next to me for the interview. I tell him more or less the same things I told Phyllis Griffiths. When he asks if I would like other girls to play hockey, I give him a straight answer.

"It's all right as long as I don't have to play on a team with girls. Girls are no good. They're always in the way of the puck. And they're too soft. If you throw snowballs at them, they cry…I'd rather play with boys. Girls have nothing in the head!"

Ben Rose seems surprised by my answer.

"But that's nothing compared to my big brothers!" I continue. "They're screwballs! They're not my idols, even though they think they are!"

Paul and Muni are somewhere in the arena; Paul with Erica, Muni with Bowden Junior, watching the figure skating.

Ben Rose changes the subject. He asks what I want to do in life.

"School teacher or prospector. But for now, I'm trying hard to score my first goal with the Tee Pees. There aren't that many games left before the end of the season."

"Usually defensemen don't score goals," he remarks.

I glance at my mother. "Mom will give me a dollar if I score a goal. I did have one clean breakaway, but the goalie blocked the shot. Of course, it's better if I stay in my position."

Encouraged by a look from the reporter, Coach Grossi offers his opinion. As if that's all he'd been waiting for.

"I defy anyone to pick her out as a girl when the team

is on the ice," he says. "Ab skates like a boy, plays aggressively, meets the players when they come in on defense. She hasn't got the speed to be a forward, but that's true of a lot of boys, too. She's improved a lot since the start of the season."

Next my mother tells Ben Rose about my first time skating at the rink in front of my house when I was three, about my desire to play hockey in the league, and about the adventures that led to the recent events.

Finally, Ben Rose puts his notebook away and thanks us. He will be watching from the bleachers while I do the interview with CBC television.

Mr. Grossi takes my mother and me to the rink. He tells me a net has been set up, away from the figure skaters, so the cameramen can shoot the hockey sequences.

Wearing a hat and a long grey coat, Mr. Henderson, the CBC journalist, explains what he wants from me. "Abby, we'd like to get some shots of you. You see the bench over there? You're going to sit and tie your skates—"

"They're already tied!"

"You can untie them, and re-tie them," he says patiently. "Then you'll skate toward the net with the puck, shoot, and come back."

Meanwhile, Susie glides toward me to say hello. "Hey, Abby, it never stops! The newspapers! The TV!"

"Abby, this is your friend?" interrupts Mr. Henderson.

I introduce him to Susie. The journalist turns to his cameraman. He has an idea. "We'd have both sports side by side. Abby, you're going to tie your skates at one end of the bench and your friend will get ready at the other end."

"Are you into it, Susie?" I ask, happy to share the limelight with someone. She's so excited, she twirls like a top.

The spotlights indicate that we're starting. I tie my skates without looking at the camera, put on my gloves, and take off toward the net. I don't pay any attention to Susie who is no longer in my field of vision. But there, standing by the net is a strange-looking girl, dressed for figure skating and holding a hockey stick! I lose my concentration, shoot, and miss! The puck hits the post and bounces to center ice.

My blunder doesn't escape Paul and Muni, who are attracted to the spotlights like moths to flames. "If you continue like this, you won't score your first goal this year," yells Paul.

"Next time, aim for the other post!" Muni adds.

I hurry to retrieve the puck. I feel like an intruder in the middle of all these girls decked out like fairy princesses. I make my way around them, slipping the puck between their legs, until I'm back in the area of the shoot.

"One more time," announces the cameraman. Mr.

Henderson comforts me by telling me that the camera can intimidate even professional players.

"One day," he says, "we were filming a Toronto Maple Leafs goalie. The players had to shoot at him and he had to make a save…in theory. In reality, it was a completely different story! Believe me, Abby, he couldn't stop a single shot. He kept saying that the spotlights were blinding him."

"What did you do?"

The cameraman chuckles at the memory. "We cheated. We asked a player to make like he was shooting at the goalie, but without the puck. Next we put the puck in the goalie's glove and shot him pretending to make a save. Then all he had to do was proudly show the puck to the camera while his teammate looked impressed."

Feeling more at ease now, we try the sequence again. This time with success. Except I got to the net a little too fast and crashed into it. Mr. Henderson invites me to join him on the bench. Just like Ben Rose and Phyllis Griffiths before him, he asks me more or less the same questions to which I give more or less the same answers.

With one exception.

It's the last question. "So, Ab, what do you think about all this attention around you?"

My hands, which I try to rest on my knees, betray my nervousness. I keep playing with my fingers. "It's complete nonsense," I say with a smile.

After hesitating for a second, Mr. Henderson bursts into laughter.

"We got it," says the cameraman.

On the other side of the boards, a trio is waiting for the next step: my mother, Chairman Graham in his dark suit, and Coach Grossi. I join them. My mother has brought my coat from the locker room.

"We won't see your skates, Abby," explains the cameraman. "Seeing you off the ice, in your everyday clothes, will give us a different perspective."

Mr. Henderson positions us according to the order of his questions: my mother and me on the right, Earl Graham in the middle, and Al Grossi on the left. Since he's conducting the interview from the ice, we're a little higher than he is.

To my mother, who seems larger than life, he asks, "How do you feel about your daughter playing hockey in a boys' league?"

My mother is calm. "Our family loves hockey. You know, at this age, sport is as beneficial for girls as it is for boys."

To Mr. Graham: "As chairman of the league, what was your reaction when you learned the truth about Abby?"

Mr. Graham answers, "I was completely shocked! I didn't think it was possible to find a girl among the four hundred boys in our league. We had to make a decision fast. Abby was allowed to play in the league, like the boys, but with one difference. She was given a private room in which to change." He exchanges a glance with my mother...

To Al Grossi: "You're the coach of Abby's team."

It's not really a question but Mr. Grossi is already smiling, thinking about what he's going to say.

"Ab has become a good player. I'm a little embarrassed when I think about the number of times I yelled at her to crush guys against the boards!"

"Thank you all," concludes the journalist.

Chapter 19

This morning, three new clippings are pinned to the board in the kitchen.

One from the *Toronto Daily Star*, has the headline "No Time For Girls—Abby" by Ben Rose. After reading it, I realize that I went overboard when I said "Girls have nothing in the head." However, I take full responsibility for what was written about my brothers.

"Yes! You're screwballs and you're absolutely not my idols!" I say, noticing that they're offended by that passage in the article.

"I don't want to hear you call me a screwball all day, Abigail Golda Hoffman," grumbles Paul.

"You deserve it!"

"You're being unfair! We're always encouraging you," laments Muni.

"No, you're always discouraging me!"

Only one photo was printed in the *Star*: the one where I'm in the classic pose of a hockey player. Too bad the one with Little Benny playing hockey in front of me didn't make the cut.

One of the articles makes me especially happy. Written by Phyllis Griffiths and in the *Toronto Telegram*, it is titled "A Girl Hockey League." I read that one day, I'll wear lipstick.

Really? This intriguing beginning takes us straight to the heart of the subject. Because of me, or thanks to me, depending on the point of view, the officials of the Little Toronto Hockey League had the idea of asking around to see if there were other Abby Hoffmans out there. "Frankly, no one knows," the article says. "But there had to be girls who play hockey in outdoor rinks, or in schoolyards, or on frozen ponds. Some of them, like Abby, may have big brothers who inspired them."

"See?" exclaims Paul, pointing at the article. "Muni and I are your idols. Stop denying it. Phyllis mentioned it again!"

"Norman Sharp, the president of the league, has an eleven year-old son, Matthew, who plays with the Toronto Marlboros in the Little Toronto Hockey League. He also has a nine-year-old daughter, Margaret, who wants to play.

"Ralph Barber, the Registrar, has a nine-year-old daughter, Susanne, who is pestering him about giving hockey a try.

"Al Grossi, the Tee Pees coach, knows that his seven-year-old daughter, Marilyn, would like to play and so would her friend Mary-Claire, who is just six.

"For more information on what has transpired over the last twenty-four hours," Phyllis continues, "girls should contact Earl Graham, chairman of the Little Toronto Hockey League, at Varsity Arena next Saturday between 5:00 and 8:00 p.m. In the following month, the ice will be available for games every Friday night from 6:00 to 8:00 p.m. If there are enough girls to make four teams, a league will be created."

To conclude, Phyllis mentions that not so long ago, "...women's hockey in Toronto was more or less dying because of girls' lack of interest for the sport. It disappeared amidst mocking at girls who had taken up hockey too late to learn how to skate, brake, handle the puck, and shoot with skill. Today, there are only a handful of private schools where girls can play. But now the Toronto Hockey League wants to attract them younger, like Abby."

"You see, Abby? All of this is thanks to you," Mom tells me.

"You're a star," adds Dad.

He's quoting the title of Phyllis Griffiths's second *Telegram* article.

She writes that my story is one of the most heart-warming incidents to figure in the news lately. She talks about my teammates' surprise when they discovered my secret. Yet they all expressed the desire that I stay on the team to finish the season.

She also mentions that I made a name for myself and she says that, like thousands of readers in Toronto, she hopes I can continue my hockey career.

"Abby has triumphed in a sport in which girls rarely compete, but there always have to be pioneers in these matters. Best of luck, Ab. The Tee Pees feel they can't get along without you. Who knows but in 10 or 12 years Ab could be the first girl player in the National Hockey League."

"I think Phyllis likes you a lot," says Dad, while trying to knot his tie.

My mother comes to his aid.

"Should I tell Phyllis that my brothers are not my idols, and that they're screwballs?"

"You can tell her tomorrow night," Mom replies with a smile.

Paul sticks his head out of the bathroom, his toothbrush in his mouth. "Is she coming for dinner?"

Muni shows up behind him. He's combing his hair even though he has a crew cut.

"We'll tell her that we're your idols and that you owe us respect!"

Little Benny sits on my father's foot and grabs his leg. "Take me around, Dad."

My father walks around the table, dragging his son as if he were dragging a ball and chain.

"No, Phyllis is not coming here tomorrow. We're meeting her at Maple Leaf Gardens. The Maple Leafs have invited us to a game against the New York Rangers."

This news is met with whoops of joy. Paul, Muni, and I regularly attend the games of the St. Catharines Tee Pees. But seeing a game in the National Hockey League will be a first!

All of a sudden, I think about my weekend, about all the activities that fill the board in our kitchen. Tonight, we're having dinner at my grandparents' place so we can watch the CBC news segment on television. Saturday afternoon, my team is playing the St. Michael's Majors. Then in the evening, we've been invited by the Maple Leafs. And Sunday, I'll serve as the mascot of the Junior Tee Pees at the Gardens.

It almost makes me dizzy.

●

At school, nobody is prouder than Mr. Williams, our principal. He shows up in our classroom first thing in the morning. The students are sitting on the carpet, watching and learning how to make crystals from sugar and water. The principal has copies of the morning newspapers, including the *Toronto Telegram* and the *Toronto Daily Star*, tucked under his arm. All the attention is on me, and it's starting to make me terribly uncomfortable.

Mr. Williams notices newspaper clippings pinned to our bulletin board. "Ms. Morley, I see that you're aware of our Abby's accomplishments, and that you have shared them with the students."

"Yes," answers my teacher. "The children actually brought in the newspapers."

Two girls, Norma and Jane, raise their hands. "Thank you, young ladies," says the principal.

A few boys next to me sigh in irritation. My success may provoke admiration amongst girls, but it can have the opposite effect on boys, most of whom don't understand this sudden infatuation for me. I tend to agree with them. I really haven't accomplished anything other than to play hockey.

The principal spreads the newspapers out on our teacher's desk. "If you don't mind," he says. He leafs through one of them, looking for an article. Suddenly, his face lights up. His taps the page with his finger. "Here it is!"

Mr. Williams holds up the page for all the students to see. I recognize the photo published in the *Telegram*. It's the one where you see me from head to toe, wearing my Tee Pees jersey, with the name on my stick prominent in the foreground.

However, the article is shorter and the title is different: "Great Pretender: Girl, 9, Hockey Ace." My name is not even mentioned. Just…girl!

The principal reads the article. After the first few words, he stops and throws a boy, Stephen, out of the classroom. He caught him dozing off. "You! To my office!" he commands. " I'll make sure that you stay awake for the rest of the day."

We shiver in fear. The principal is known for his harsh punishment.

The article, which he reads in one fell swoop, almost without breathing, is familiar. It's a long summary of Phyllis Griffiths's first *Telegram* article.

I mention this to him.

"You're right, Abby. But this is not published in a Toronto newspaper." He shows us the front page of *the paper.*

"It's in *The New York Times!*" he shouts, choked by emotion. Aside from the teacher, no one reacts. Whether it's the *Times* or the *Telegram,* a newspaper is a newspaper.

No one reveals that they only know the city because of the hockey team—the New York Rangers. Someone should remind the principal that he's talking to nine-year-olds, not to their parents. As if he's just remembered a detail, the principal continues.

"They also wrote about you in Montreal—in *La Presse*."

I know that Montreal is in Canada. That's easy: the Montreal Canadiens. The Rangers should be called the New York Americans. It would make it easier for us young hockey fans, to remember that New York is in the United States.

The principal hands *The New York Times* to Ms. Morley. "You can put it up on your board. Have a great day!"

The class falls silent again. I'm more preoccupied with the fate of poor Stephen, who must be quivering in fear in the principal's office, than with my appearance in the newspapers of North America.

———

It's hard for me to forget that I'm the girl who plays hockey with boys.

In the early afternoon, our class visits the Royal Ontario Museum in downtown Toronto. I love that place. I go every month with Paul to meetings of the Young Naturalists Club of Toronto.

In one of the natural history galleries on level two, we're admiring a triceratops's skull when a group of students from another school enters. Suddenly, I feel several pairs of eyes on me. I hear barely contained whispers.

"I swear, it's him!"

"You mean her!"

A little voice shouts: "It's Abby Hoffman!"

Young strangers, who have eyes only for me, sur-round me. Too bad for the triceratops, although I doubt it minds. What should I do? Greet them? Flee?

A lady introduces herself. She's the group's teacher. "So you're Abby Hoffman?"

I nod.

She shows me her camera. "Can we take a picture of you with our class? It would make a wonderful souve-nir, especially since we read all the articles about you this week."

"Yesss!" applaud the kids, excited.

"Wouldn't you prefer a picture with our three-horned friend?" I ask, indicating the dinosaur.

"Nooo!" the kids cry out. They squeeze together to be as close to me as possible. I notice that the majority of them are girls. The boys, standing to the side, prefer the triceratops's head to mine. I can't blame them.

I'm overwhelmed with requests for autographs. The museum, usually so calm and quiet, suddenly becomes noisy, alerting the guard. He limps over to us. "Not so loud!" he scolds. "You're going to wake up the dinosaurs!"

Ms. Morley, who had already moved to the next room, realizes that I'm the indirect cause of all this racket. Excuse me," she says, making her way to me. "Abby needs to continue her visit for her school work."

Good try, but what she hadn't anticipated was that the whole group would want to continue with me!

Chapter 20

The activities planned for today are so exciting that we wouldn't dream of sleeping in, except for Little Benny, who has a high temperature and a runny nose. My grandparents, with whom we watched the CBC news segment last night, have agreed to watch him until tomorrow. Who knows what time I'll go to bed this evening…or tonight?

What a Saturday! There's the prize draw—shoulder pads, a jersey, a stick and a puck—for the best ticket sellers. Then our team plays the St. Michael's Majors in the last game of the regular season, a game where I would really like to score my first goal. And tonight is the game between Toronto and the New York Rangers at Maple

Leaf Gardens. A real game with real players from the National Hockey League that I'll watch with my brothers—if they're nice—my parents, and other guests.

A lot of people read the newspaper stories, but even more people watch TV! When I arrive at Varsity Arena for our Saturday afternoon game, a welcome committee greets me. A dozen girls, skates in hand or hung around their necks, want to meet me. Since the hallway leading to the locker room is not very wide, they're blocking the way. Judging by their toothless smiles, some of these girls are younger than me. The majority, however, are my brothers' ages.

Seven-year-old twins, Barbara and Bonnie—cute brunettes with freckles on their faces—tell me that they want to register in the future girls' league. "Do you have any advice for us?"

The others, who were cackling like hens two seconds ago, go quiet, wait for what I'm about to say. I'll give the twins a straight answer. "Your skates…they're girl skates, for figure skating."

"So?" says Barbara—or is it Bonnie?

"Playing hockey is not like jumping or doing pirouettes! You need boy skates, like these." I show them the skates that my brothers wore before me. "That's the first step in the right direction."

My mother apologizes and pushes through the group. "Abby can't be late for her game."

She takes me to Chairman Graham's office where I need to change. The door is locked! How stupid! And the Tee Pees locker room is right next door.

"Is there a problem, Ab?" asks Jim Halliday, who has already put on his jersey and skates. He's always the first to arrive and the last to leave. I explain the situation.

Jim doesn't consult Mr. Grossi, not this time, anyway. He points to the team's locker room. "We'll close our eyes when you put on your skates," he jokes.

With a little tap on the shoulder, my mother encourages me to go. "If I bump into one of the gentlemen, I'll tell them what happened."

She thanks Jim. "You're a good captain, young man. You show great initiative, and you're intelligent and generous."

Jim is pleased with the compliments. I follow him into the locker room. The Tee Pees acknowledge my presence with screams and whistles.

"Aaaah! A girl!" exclaims Scotty. He crosses his arms in front of him to hide his jersey. "Look away, Hoffman! I'm indecent," he says trying to ridicule me.

"I'm happy to see you too, Scotty."

I'm bombarded with questions and comments about my appearance in the newspapers and on television. I notice that the articles have been pinned to the bulletin board.

"You said something in the articles I agree with, Hoffman," says Scotty.

I'm shocked. "Well, that would be a first," I reply.

"It's true that girls have nothing in their heads. You're the living proof."

I tell him that I also included a certain bespectacled teammate as being part of that empty-headed group, but that the reporter ignored my comment. "It's too bad because you would have finally seen your name in the paper."

I slip on my skates with pleasure. There's something so satisfying about putting on your equipment with your team. Alone in Earl Graham's office the other day, I felt like I didn't belong to the Tee Pees anymore. I hope the chairman doesn't catch me—he'll send me back to his office for sure.

"Ah! The entire team is here!" remarks Coach Grossi as he enters the room. "Perfect!"

But Chairman Graham, who appears right behind him, doesn't share that opinion. Strangely, when he's away from the TV cameras, he doesn't wear his Sunday smile. He turns to me. "Shouldn't you be in my office?"

"The door was locked! Didn't my mother tell you?"

His eyes are shifty. "I didn't see your mother."

"Abby changed in the showers. There was no one there," assures Jim Halliday, quick to come to my rescue.

"That's not true! I was there! I was washing!" claims Scotty. He's so twisted.

Graham Powell looks up. He just finished rolling tape seventeen times around the blade of his stick, a ritual he repeats at every game. "That's impossible, Hynek. You never wash. We're going to tell your father!"

The Tee Pees crack up, which has the unintended effect of driving the chairman out of the room. The coach closes the door so his team won't be bothered anymore. "Gentlemen," he starts, "and lady, this is the last game of our regular season. Our current standing is four wins and four losses; it would be nice to end on a positive note before the playoffs. Let's try hard to make that happen. Tonight, we also have the prize draw for players who sold tickets to support the league's activities next year so—"

"Don't kid yourself, Hoffman. I'm going to win, I'm sure of it," whispers Scotty.

"How many tickets did you sell?"

"One…actually, my parents bought it."

"One book of ten tickets?"

"No! Hoffman, are you crazy? One single ticket. That's all you need to win. You? Did you sell any?"

"Me? Thirty—"

"Thirty tickets? Your parents ruined themselves for nothing."

"Thirty books, Scotty! And my parents only bought one!"

Coach Grossi continues his speech. "The prize will be drawn by Chairman Graham right before the game. And there will be a team photo after the meet. So wait a bit before you go back to the locker room."

"Is it for the newspaper?" asks Scotty, somewhat hopeful.

"It's for *The New York Times*," I tell him.

"No," answers Mr. Grossi. "It's a souvenir for you and your parents."

Suddenly, the siren resonates through Varsity Arena. "Game time!" calls Al Grossi. The Tee Pees jump to their feet. "By the way," he warns us, "there are a lot of people this afternoon."

Usually when we enter the rink, we dart to our zone and pay no attention to the opposing team or to our families in the bleachers. But none of us are looking at the ice right now. Our entrance has caused an uproar. It so terrified Scotty, who was first in line, that he scampered off, jumped the boards, and took refuge on our bench.

The noise is deafening, like for the Junior Tee Pees games, which usually attract thousands of spectators. But today, they're all here for us, for nine- and ten-year-old kids!

A little reassured, Scotty comes back on the ice. "This is all because of you, Hoffman!" he complains.

"This *is* all thanks to you, Abby!" says David Kurtis,

excited at the idea of playing his favorite sport in front of such a huge crowd.

I don't dare look up at the bleachers. From the corner of my eye, I see the girls who welcomed me in the hallway earlier. They're chanting my name.

Has a warm-up at Varsity Arena ever been this loud?

With the announcement of the draw, calm returns to the arena. The two teams go to their respective benches. Standing at center ice, Chairman Graham digs into a large glass drum filled with little pieces of white paper folded in half. He rotates the drum a few times, fumbles around, and grabs one piece at random.

The announcer hands him the microphone so he can reveal who, among the league players who sold tickets, will be receiving the prize. He silently reads the name, and then his face lights up with surprise.

"Well! It's her week!"

"Abby," David whispers to me, "you won!"

Mr. Graham looks in our direction.

"It's me!" cries Scotty. "It's me! It's…"

"Abby Hoffman!" announces the chairman.

As I leave the bench, Scotty launches into a rant about how unfair it is that Abby sold more tickets than he did.

The crowd gives me a huge ovation. Not so much because they're happy that I won the prize; I think it's more to acknowledge my year among the boys. Oh, if only I could score a goal to thank them!

Mr. Graham offers me the Maple Leafs jersey, a puck, a stick, and shoulder pads. He grabs my hand for the photograph. "You can pick up your stuff in my office—where you usually change—after the game," he says without losing his smile.

Understood.

Back on the bench, my fellow Tee Pees congratulate me. But not Scotty—big surprise—who is too busy sulking at the end of the bench. I approach and hand him the puck.

"Here, big baby!"

He looks at me, stunned. "I'd rather have the stick, Hoffman."

Coach Grossi sends his first forward line and his first pair of defensemen—David and me—on the ice.

Cheered by the enthusiastic crowd, we play our best game of the season. The Tee Pees win easily 5-0 against the St. Michael's Majors. The Majors can't help but be intimidated by this crowd that roots for the Tee Pees throughout the entire game.

Captain Halliday distinguishes himself with a hat trick. I get an assist on one of those goals, my third point of the season. We were in the enemy zone with me positioned at the blue line. An opponent tried to bounce the puck against the boards to clear the zone. I intercepted it on the line, preventing an offside and allowing the attack to go on. I hit a wrist shot low on the ice. The puck slipped between the players' skates and landed on the blade of Halliday's stick. Before their goalie had time to react, the puck was already behind him.

After Halliday's goal was announced—his third— the rink was inundated with hats to mark the hat trick. But when the announcer added "with an assist from number six, Ab Hoffman," the intensity of the cheers doubled. That's an unusual reaction given how important the goal scorer is.

Like me, Scotty also failed to score his first goal. He missed a great opportunity during a breakaway toward the net. Distracted by all the cheering, he lost the puck while trying to outsmart the goalie. He was so irritated with himself that he didn't gather with us around our goalie after the game. Worse, he went straight to the locker room, skipping the team photograph. Jim Halliday had to go get him and practically drag him by the ear.

For the photo, I was placed in the front row, second from the left, with one knee on the ice. Scotty's mood shifted for the better. He even went to the trouble of removing his glasses.

"Ready?" calls out the photographer. "Say...Abby!"

"Abbyyyyy!"

Standing behind me, Scotty opts for "Scottyyyyy" instead.

There's a surprise waiting for the players in the locker room. But not for me. With the chairman watching me like a cat watches a mouse, I have no choice but to change in his office. I slip my prizes into a bag and hurry back to my teammates.

The coach had waited for me before talking to his protégés. "As you know, our famous Ab is in fact an Abby. She's been invited to the Maple Leafs game against the Rangers at the Gardens tonight."

"We're very happy for her," Scotty Hynek quips snidely while putting away the puck I gave him.

"Abby accepted the gift from the Leafs, but on one condition." All eyes swing back and forth between Mr. Grossi and me.

"The condition is that all the Tee Pees go with her."

The locker room erupts in cheers. I'm lifted onto a pair of shoulders for a lap of honor round the room. And then it's my turn to be stunned. One of the shoulders supporting me is…Scotty's!

Chapter 21

Though the game between the Rangers and the Leafs doesn't start until 8:00 p.m., I want to arrive at the Gardens early. So I wolf down my dinner as quickly as possible. No time to waste on a meal.

My family and I meet up with Phyllis Griffiths in the lobby. It's thanks to her that we got tickets for the whole team tonight.

Phyllis gives my parents and my brothers their tickets. We're not all sitting in the same section. I'll be with Phyllis because I have an assignment to describe, in an article, my experience watching my first National Hockey League game. Actually, Phyllis will write the article after observing and questioning me, and she'll send it to me so I can approve it. Thank goodness, because otherwise it would feel like I was doing homework all weekend.

I can't wait for this evening to start. It's amazing what a simple 'F' on a birth certificate has done over the last few weeks.

When Phyllis and I enter the rink, there's almost no one there, on the ice or in the bleachers. The ice is beautiful and smooth, without any blade marks. We're standing at ice level. I can hardly look at the rows all the way to the top without breaking my neck. The place is huge, at least three times as big as Varsity Arena where I usually play.

Phyllis points out something as we head toward our seats. We're going by the players' benches where big butts from New York and Toronto will soon be parked. The benches have cushions! Our bench at Varsity is not as comfortable. It doesn't even compare; it's all wood, not at all easy on our bony posteriors.

With Phyllis's permission, I sit on the Leafs' bench and look over the boards. Because of my size, I can't see a thing. Am I sitting in the spot where, in about an hour, George Armstrong will be sitting? Or the two Jims: Thompson and Morrison? Will Toronto ace scorer Tod Sloan sit nearby, give the referees hell, and cheer his teammates? Will he get a slap on the back from his coach, Connie Smythe?

A lady dressed in blue takes us to our seats. Amazing! We have the best seats in the arena. Phyllis shows me the program. It has the line-up for both teams and a plan of the Gardens. She points to where my parents will be sitting, very close to us; my brothers, on the other hand, will be at the top of the blue section, in front of the orchestra, which is rehearsing *God Save The Queen*.

As for the Tee Pees, they'll be in the highest section, the grays, spread out through the entire arena.

Oh, I see defenseman Tim Horton. He's leaning against the boards. Will he be the first Leaf on the ice? No. He's standing still as a statue and staring at the rink. Oh? He's drinking coffee.

"It's a ritual he does before every game," explains Phyllis. "It helps him concentrate."

Good idea. I should do the same before the Tee Pees games. Except that my parents would never let me drink coffee. Maybe tea? As soon as the Rangers step on the ice, Tim Horton retires to his locker room. The Rangers skate in circles in their zone. I feel a cool breeze brush against my face as the players whiz by.

A tall man comes up to greet Phyllis. He has a funny moustache under a large nose. She introduces me to fellow sports journalist Ted Reeve. He seems delighted.

"So you're the famous Abby Hoffman! My friend Phyl has told all of us at the newspaper so much about you!" Then he excuses himself and climbs toward the Leafs' VIP section to shake hands.

I try to identify the players by matching their

numbers with the names in the program. It would be much simpler for spectators if the players from both teams had their names as well as their numbers on the back of their jerseys.

Now it's the Leafs' turn to get on the ice. After skating around in circles for a minute or two, George Armstrong drops a bunch of pucks in his zone so his teammates can shoot at goalie Johnny Bower.

"Watch out!"

One of the Toronto players—I don't know which one—threw a shot that almost hit Bower in the face. At the last second, Bower protected himself with his glove. He's now chewing out Tim Horton, number 7.

The two teams keep going for about fifteen minutes before returning to their locker rooms. Then, as the Gardens fills up, the Zamboni comes out to do its job. My parents have just made it to their seats. And my brothers? Yes, they're up there! I signal to them that I have a very good seat, thank you very much! Judging by their faces, they're dying of envy.

There's no point in trying to find the Tee Pees; they're lost in the densely packed crowd. As usual, this Saturday night game is sold out. Sixteen thousand spectators are crammed into the Gardens.

I fill the pre-game time by eating popcorn and answering Phyllis's initial questions. When the two teams jump on the ice, a strange and loud mix of booing for the Rangers and cheering for the Leafs greets them. A cacophony, as Mom would call it.

It doesn't get quiet again until the teams have lined up on their respective blue lines for the orchestra's rendition of *God Save The Queen*. A spotlight comes on over a giant portrait of Queen Elizabeth hanging from the ceiling.

Hey! I see a man over there, in one of the blue seats at the north end, who forgot to remove his hat!

The game starts. It's so fast, I can hardly follow it. The Rangers score early. While I'm writing down the name of the scorer in my program, a collective sigh of disappointment fills the arena. The visitors scored a second goal and I didn't even see it!

Since the Leafs are behind by two goals so early in the game, I'm convinced they won't get anywhere. They lost 4-3 against the Canadiens two days ago. At the end of first period, they're still lagging 2-0.

At the intermission, my parents join Phyllis and me.

"It's very strange to watch tall men play hockey," says Mom.

"Dorothy, you've seen so many games in the Little Hockey League that you can't imagine players being more than five feet tall anymore," replies Dad.

My brothers come down from their perch too. They're not very happy.

"What don't you like?" I ask them. "The game or your seats?"

"No, Abby. It's not that," answers Paul, annoyed. "Some girls heard that we were your brothers and they asked us for an autograph."

"And that's why you're grumpy?" Mom admonishes.

"No," says Muni. "The girls read the *Star* article, the one by Ben Rose—sorry, Phyllis—and they asked that next to our names we write…screwballs!"

Their troubles don't bother me in the least. It's true that I called them screwballs, but I never thought anyone would remember.

An older couple stops by to congratulate me. I thank them and introduce my parents, and my two screwball brothers. Offended, my brothers climb back up to the last row of the blues. The siren announces the end of the intermission. People return to their seats to make sure they don't miss any of the action.

The players are in position for second period face off, but the referee keeps the puck in his hand. He seems to be waiting for something, a signal maybe. He's looking toward the penalty bench.

The announcer's voice comes on: "The officials of the Toronto Maple Leafs would like to welcome a very special guest tonight—a nine-year-old girl from our city, who plays hockey in a boys' league."

Hey! They're talking about me!

"Ladies and Gentlemen, please give a round of applause for the young Abby Hoffman!"

The spotlight that was focused on the queen's face earlier is now on me! The crowd gives me a standing ovation.

"You should stand up and acknowledge the public," Phyllis suggests quietly.

With my heart beating at 200 miles an hour, I obey. Then I sit down as abruptly as I stood up. *Did I smile? I can't remember.*

The referee's whistle puts an end to my tribute. After all, I'm only a girl who plays hockey, and there's a game on tonight. That's perfectly fine by me. Phyllis hands me my program and I concentrate on the game that's starting again.

The Leafs redouble their efforts. Our coach always tells us that we can't give up until it's over, and that's exactly how the Leafs seem to think. It's as if Al Grossi and Connie Smythe use the same tactics to shake up their team.

In less than ten minutes, the Leafs score three goals! It's now 3-2.

At the beginning of the game, I didn't know what team to root for. My favorite team will always be the Detroit Red Wings. But swept up in the electrifying atmosphere of the Gardens, I scream and whistle for the Leafs.

Watching the Toronto defensemen—mainly Thompson, Morrison, Stewart, and Horton—I learn a lot of tricks about how to play my position. The only difference is that these guys skate backwards about thirty times faster than me. It'll take me another two or three years before I can catch up with them.

I also like forward Tod Sloan. He's the Leafs' best player. He scored the third goal in second period—his 37th of the season. He matched the record for the highest number of goals scored by a Toronto player in a year, says Phyllis, who never misses a thing.

Third period belongs to the Leafs, who score two more goals. I note the goals, assists, and penalties in my program. When I play with the Tee Pees, my mother gives me fifty cents for an assist and a dollar for a goal.

I scream the last seconds of the countdown with thousands of happy Leaf fans. At the sound of the siren, the winners receive a well-deserved standing ovation. Everybody leaves with a smile—they had a great evening.

The lady dressed in blue—the one who seated us when we first arrived—comes back to get us. The Leafs have invited me to their locker room to meet the players! Spiff Evans, the team's publicist, organized this visit, Phyllis tells me.

I search the crowd for Paul and Muni, but without success. The lady politely explains that we don't have much time because the players have to get on a train to New York to play the Rangers again tomorrow night.

My parents decide to wait for my brothers so I go

with Phyllis and the lady in blue. In the hallway leading to the locker room, the lady hands me over to the publicist. I hear the winners cheering on the other side of the door.

While Phyllis stands off to the side, Spiff Evans opens the door. The players are happy. They look like us when we win a game. With only one difference—we haven't started sweating under our arms yet. The two players Mr. Evans introduces me to—the two Jims, Thompson and Morrison—are dripping with sweat. Quick, a shower!

I sit down between them. They both crush my hand in a handshake.

"How are you doing, Abigail?" asks Thompson. "You've been in the paper a lot over the last few days."

I'm so star-struck that all I can manage is a dumb smile. I'm sure my brothers would love to see me like this more often.

A player I don't know comes by. He's not wearing his Leafs jersey, but a completely drenched, short-sleeve undershirt.

"Hi, son…"

"Hey! She's a girl," the two Jims reply.

Confused, the player withdraws his hand and walks away muttering, "Girls are bad luck in a locker room."

"I apologize for him, Abby," says Morrison, looking embarrassed. "That moron has been hit in the head one too many times."

Thompson, who knows the Tee Pees are playing the Hamilton Cubs next Friday, gives me some tricks to block an attack. "If an opponent charges at you, don't worry about the puck," he advises. "Handle him like a man, Abby," continues Morrison, "and shove him against the boards!"

I manage to recover my ability to speak. "Yes, thank you."

Before leaving to go freshen up, they wish me good luck and give me autographed programs for my team-mates. Spiff Evans makes sure the photographer captures the scene.

Then Mr. Evans takes me to Tod Sloan. I walk by George Armstrong who's talking to three journalists. He looks terrible—in the second period, he took a puck to his upper lip. He needed four stiches to repair the damage, Spiff Evans tells me.

Tod Sloan welcomes me with kind words. He hasn't taken off his Leafs jersey, the one with the big A, for Assistant Captain, embroidered on the heart side. I ask him: "Do you have sticks to sell? I'm sure it would help me score my first goal."

Tod does even better. He gives me his own stick! For free! He writes his name on it and hands me two pucks, under the eye of the photographer snapping shots for the newspaper.

The Leafs's star player then apologizes; he needs to

get going so he can change and make his train to New York. He too crushes my hand in a hearty handshake.

I drop a puck on the floor—the one that's not new—and I handle it with the stick. The stick is way too long. By at least twelve inches. If I want to use it, I'll have to cut it shorter. Either that or keep it as a souvenir. Or I could give it to Muni, who's a big fan of Tod Sloan.

On the way out, I bump into Mr. Smythe, the Leafs coach. Spiff Evans introduces me: "Mr. Smythe, this is Abigail Hoffman, the girl who is a star defenseman in a hockey league for boys."

He crushes my hand and looks at me in a strange way. "Excellent, good for you…"

Phyllis Griffiths addresses him. "Remember her name. You never know, the Leafs may need a good defenseman sometime in the future," she tells him.

"If I forget, I count on you to remind me," he answers, visibly preoccupied by more important things. He says good-bye and disappears into the locker room.

My parents catch up with us, and I show them the souvenirs that the players gave me.

"Hey! Look what I got!" shouts Paul, as excited as if he had won five shutout victories in a row. He holds up a goalie stick. "Gump Worsley gave it to me. He was talking to a journalist in the hallway. I told him he was my favorite goalie and that I'd never seen anyone go from a vertical to a horizontal position as fast as him.

He laughed, then apologized and disappeared into the Rangers locker room.

"I thought our conversation was over. But no! He came back ten seconds later and gave me his autographed stick!"

"And I don't have anything!" complains Muni.

I hand him Tod Sloan's stick. "For you! For wearing the dress at the restaurant." Muni is so happy that he does something he hasn't done in ages: he kisses me on the cheek.

Yuk!

Chapter 22

I think I fell asleep with both pucks under my pillow.
"If the Tooth Fairy had looked under there last night,
she would have had quite a surprise," teases Paul.

"Not as much as with Muni!" I say. "He slept with
Tod Sloan's stick!"

The atmosphere is relaxed at the Hoffmans on this
Sunday morning, the day after the Leafs game. What an
adventure!

But my weekend is not over yet.

●

I'm back at Maple Leaf Gardens, not to see the Leafs
who left last night for New York, but to be the mascot

for the Junior Tee Pees. They are playing the Toronto Marlboros in the Ontario Junior Hockey League semi-finals. The Marlboros are leading the series 3-1. Another win and they're going to the finals.

Last year, the Tee Pees won the Memorial Cup—a trophy that honors the best junior team in Canada. I remember there was a parade on the streets of St. Catharines in the spring. The Tee Pees were sitting in convertible cars. A young player from the Little Toronto Hockey League, wearing the Tee Pees colors, accompanied each one of them.

I can already see myself, sitting next to assistant captain Ab McDonald, the sun shining, both of us waving to thousands of fans. They'd scream "Ab! Ab!" and I would think they were talking to me!

I hope to bring good luck to the junior team because Ab McDonald, who has a great memory, didn't forget about meeting in the hallway of Varsity Arena. He had suggested I be their team mascot for this game at Maple Leaf Gardens.

I'm supposed to bring my hockey equipment to the event, including skates and stick.

When my parents and I arrive at the Gardens, we go in through the players' entrance. (Muni and Paul, who arranged to meet his Erica Westbrook, are already somewhere in the arena.) A bald man leads us to an empty locker room so I can put on my skates. "I'll come back in a few minutes to get you, Ab," he informs me.

I just have time to tie my laces and he's back with a Tee Pees player—the captain, Elmer Vasko. He's a giant! His assistant captain, Ab McDonald, and a photographer are right behind him.

Ab introduces me to Elmer, nicknamed Moose, and mentions that a photo will be taken for the *Star*. I stand next to him, intimidated.

"Look at each other," says the photographer, his eye glued to the viewfinder.

"It hurts my neck!" I say.

It doesn't work for the photographer either. Elmer is so tall that my head is at the level of his hockey pants.

Ab McDonald suggests we put me up on a table.

My father drags a small table from the center of the room. Elmer and Ab each grab me by an elbow and boost me up onto the table. Ah, much better! I can now look the Moose in the eye.

"You know, Abigail," says Captain Vasko, "you and I are both Tee Pees!"

"That's true!"

But though we have the same team name on the front of our jerseys, it's not written in the same way. And the junior team jersey has the drawing of a hockey player between the Tee and the Pee.

From my perch, I compare our equipment. I'm sure Elmer doesn't wear his big brothers' skates. And his stockings don't have holes at the knees.

Before leaving, Elmer and Ab lightly hit my pads with their sticks. "For luck!" says the captain.

I don't take off my equipment. After about ten minutes, cheers from the crowd indicate that the players are on the ice. I thought for a second that I would be invited to skate with them during the warm-up. But the contrast between these big guys and me would have been too much. I can imagine the comments: the Tee Pees need a girl to face the Marlies.

Apparently, there are more than 8,000 spectators present. They're noisier than the fans who usually attend the Leaf games. A folding chair has been set up for me, next to the Tee Pees bench. From there, I can cheer them on.

I can hear Coach Rudy Pilous' instructions. In the end, they're very similar to what our coach shouts at us: "Skate! Skate!" "Watch your man!" "Hey referee, open your eyes!"

Things are not going well for the big Tee Pees. The Marlboros are all over the ice and always first on the puck; they're aggressive, powerful. It's as if the Tee Pees have their feet stuck in cement. At the end of first period, the Marlboros lead 4-0. They dominated so strongly in the first twenty minutes of the game that it's a good thing Roy Edwards, the Tee Pee goalie, was so strong. Otherwise the gap would be much greater.

The Tee Pees retire to their locker room to lick their wounds and come up with a strategy to bounce back. As for me, I sit in my chair and wait for the Zamboni to finish polishing the ice. Once the machine has gone back to its cave, the announcer's voice fills the Gardens.

"Ladies and Gentlemen, please welcome the star defenseman of the young St. Catharines Tee Pees, the sensational Abigail Hoffman!"

I pray I don't fall when I step on the ice. That would be too embarrassing. The crowd applauds with enthusiasm.

Without looking at the fans, I go around the rink once. At the Tee Pees bench, the equipment attendant gives me a puck that I drop in front of me. I go around again, handling the puck. This time, I slow down so I don't lose it. But it still escapes me twice.

I brake at the Marlies blue line, hit a wrist shot toward the net, and the puck slides into the net, setting off the red light. I raised my arms in triumph, happy and relieved to have hit the target on my first try. The announcer shouts:

"She shoots, she scores!"

The audience cheers.

"The St. Catharines Tee Pees goal was scored, with no assist, by number 6, Abby Hoffman!"

I'm thrilled. *Put that in your pipe, Scotty Hynek!*

My minute of glory comes to an end when the

players from both teams emerge from the hallway. This is my cue to leave the ice. Already, people are shifting their attention to the Tee Pees and Marlboros.

I go back to the St. Catharines bench. The guys seem tense. The referee drops the puck to start the second period.

Except for a few hiccups, the Marlboros remain in the lead. The Tee Pees score two goals by McDonald, but Toronto counters with two more goals in less than a minute.

Lagging 6-2, the Tee Pees have a lot to do to catch up.

I don't need my skates for the second intermission. I take off my equipment, put on my boots and, with my parents in tow, start the long climb toward the Gardens ceiling. An employee of the arena is taking me to an interview with a local radio station, which is broadcasting the game live.

We have to hurry because there are several flights of stairs ahead of us. As we go up, people recognize me and call my name. When I finally reach the last row of seats, out of breath—although not as much as my parents—I glance back at the rink. Ants!

"He's waiting for you, Abby," the employee insists.

I still have to climb a narrow set of stairs, cross a suspended bridge—*don't look down!*—and make it up a vertical ladder. The ladder leads to a gondola, a kind of glass cage from where the commentator describes the games. That's where the employee abandons me.

"Don't worry. If you fall, I'll catch you," he says as he leaves.

What a nasty joke! My mother gives him a piece of her mind. But she too will keep her feet solidly on the ground, because she suffers from vertigo. My father is the only one who follows me up the ladder.

He's two rungs below me, bracing me with his strong arms. No more danger of falling.

The ladder leads to one end of the gondola where Foster Hewitt welcomes us. A few minutes ago, when we were climbing the stairs, the Gardens' employee told me that Mr. Hewitt has been the voice of the Maple Leafs for years. He describes all the National Hockey League games played in Toronto, on radio and television, from one ocean to the other.

He's the one who came up with the now-famous "He shoots, he scores!"

Mr. Hewitt works alone in his suspended studio. He doesn't have a microphone. He talks to his audience by phone! He takes a short pause. He cups the receiver and indicates that it will soon be my turn, and after a few seconds, he continues his monologue.

"Ladies and Gentlemen, this afternoon I have a guest whose accomplishments you may have read about in the paper. I'm talking about Abigail Hoffman, the nine-year-old girl who is a star player in the Little Toronto Hockey League, a league…for boys!"

He hands me the phone and encourages me to speak loudly. "Good afternoon!" I manage.

He starts the conversation with things that have been covered several times over the last few days: my beginnings, my season, the revelation of my real identity, the players' reactions, the consequences, and the usual… "How many goals have you scored with the Tee Pees, Abby?"

I grab the receiver. "No goals yet. But I'm a defenseman. I'm working hard, though, and I hope to score before the end of the year."

"Do you think the Junior Tee Pees will be able to catch up with the Marlboros in third period?"

"Yes! They're going to win 7-6 and go on to the Memorial Cup Tournament."

I couldn't have been more wrong. Not only did the Tee Pees prove incapable of scoring a single goal, but also the Marlboros slammed the puck into their net one last time. Final score: 7-2.

I'm disappointed, both for the players and for myself. I didn't bring them luck. Their season is over. Despite the pain of the loss, Ab McDonald comes to see me after the game to thank me for being there.

"We needed you in the line-up, Abby. We played so badly."

There will be no car parade with me sitting next to him. My mother, who is solidly grounded, brings me back to reality.

"Tomorrow, it's back to normal life, Abby. And to school!"

Phyllis Griffiths, who was covering the game for the *Telegram*, meets up with us in the Gardens lobby as spectators make their way out. She tells us that the officials of the Little Toronto Hockey League are very happy about all the attention the media is showering on me. It will help publicize the all-star game that's taking place in two weeks at Varsity Arena.

"They expect a good turnout and they believe the money raised from the game will be enough to allow them to continue their activities next year," she declares. "The officials are also happy my story got forty girls— including three pairs of twins," she notes with a smile, "interested in playing hockey.

"Your friend Chairman Graham," she says, teasing, "announced that there will be a hockey school for girls at Varsity Arena, three evenings a week, starting Thursday, March 22nd. And all of this, thanks to you, Abigail Golda Hoffman!"

THIRD PERIOD

From March 12, 1956 to March 24, 1956

Chapter 23

As my mother said on Sunday, life is back to normal with my return to class on Monday morning.

I'm happy to see Susie Read in Ms. Morley's class.

"Hey, Abby, I watched us on television Friday night," she says, still excited.

"How were we?"

"We were brilliant!" she exclaims. "Right, Ms. Morley?"

Looking up from her notes, the teacher uses Susie's question as an opportunity to ask the class. "Who saw Abigail on television Friday night?"

A few hands go up. But not everyone has a television at home, and not everyone watches the six o'clock news.

"I was there too," says my friend, not happy that the teacher left her out.

Ms. Morley seems surprised.

"You were in the news segment, Susie? I'm sorry, I missed you. All my attention was on Abigail." She addresses her students again. "Who saw Susie on TV?"

Other than me, no one raises hands, which annoys my best friend even more.

"I was wearing my figure skating outfit," she says, as if that clue could jolt people's memory.

It does make Ms. Morley react. "Oh, yes! I saw you, Susie! I'm sorry I overlooked that detail."

Susie purses her lips. According to her teacher, her appearance on TV is nothing more than a detail. Ms. Morley continues:

"Yes, Susie. You were standing by the net, with a hockey stick in your hands. It was right when Abigail shot and scored."

My friend gives up. "This country only cares about hockey!" she laments.

Not wanting to end the conversation on a bad note, Ms. Morley gives Susie an opening. "Susie, why don't you tell us about the important visit coming up at Varsity Arena next Friday…"

Susie lights up; she has so few chances to tell the class about her favorite sport. She stands up. "Wagner and Paul are two wonderful—and true—athletes! They…"

Hands shoot up, filling Susie with pride. Finally! Students are listening to what she has to say about figure skating. She points to boy in the back of the room. "Yes, Anderson?"

"What team do Wagner and Paul play for? The Maple Leafs?"

Hands go down, a sign that everyone had the same question.

They're not crummy hockey players," barks Susie. "They're a figure skating couple."

"A guy couple named Wagner and Paul?" asks another boy, chuckling with the students around him.

"You bunch of morons!" shouts Susie, about to explode. "Wagner and Paul are last names. The two athletes are Barbara Wagner and Robert Paul."

A sigh of disappointment sweeps over the class. But Ms. Morley encourages Susie to continue.

"Wagner and Paul will be guests of honor at Varsity Arena Friday night for the Little Toronto Hockey League Jamboree."

Some hockey fans have a phenomenal memory. They can remember an astonishing number of statistics about National League players and recite them as needed. In the same way, Susie, because of her interest in figure skating, can list the accomplishments of her heroes almost as if they were hers.

"Barbara Wagner and Robert Paul are members of the Figure Skating Club of Toronto. They're the Canadian Pairs Champions. They placed fifth in the last World Championship in 1956, and finished sixth in the recent Winter Olympics in Italy. People think they're going to be the reigning pair on the world scene in the years to come."

Ms. Morley thanks her for this very informative presentation.

Anderson raises his hand. "I have a question for Susie."

My friend turns to him. "At what time are they skating?"

Susie doesn't even hesitate. "At 9:40 p.m."

The boy raises his hand again.

"Another question for Susie?" asks the teacher.

No, for Abby!"

Huh. I wasn't expecting that…

"At what time is your team playing?"

I search my memory. So many things have happened in the last few days that I have a hard time keeping track. "Uh…around 9 p.m., before the figure skaters' performance."

The boy thinks about my answer for a second, then his face lights up. "Perfect! I'll come to your game and then I'll leave! I won't have to stay for the 'show.'"

I have to support Susie. After a quick glance at her, I

add: "After the dancers' performance, there will be a draw for a 21-inch television…"

"Skaters, not dancers," corrects Susie who I've seen in a better mood.

"A television?" repeats Anderson. "It might be worth staying for. We don't have one."

"You won't regret it," promises my friend.

"You're right," says Anderson. "Especially if my parents win."

Playing hockey once a week in an organized league doesn't take away from the pleasure of going to the Humberside outdoor rink.

As soon as I'm done with my homework, I put on my skates and jump on the ice. Sometimes pick-up games are already underway. Anyone can join in. All you have to do is choose a team, preferably the one that has the least players.

Or you have to arrive early and be selected by one of the two captains ruling over the rink. They're usually the two best players in the area, or the two oldest or, at the very least, the two most aggressive.

The captains determine who gets first pick. They play heads or tails, or tug-of-war but with a hockey stick instead of a rope.

When I show up at the rink, the teams haven't been

made yet. Usually, the captains know their players and start with the most experienced. But that's not what's happening tonight.

One of the captains, Wendell Hooper, beats his counterpart, Clarke Nolan, at tug-of-war. With the matter settled, the selection starts. A dozen players wait for, or dread, the verdict. Being called early is a sign of respect and admiration. Being among the last ones picked is humiliating, painful for the self-esteem. I know exactly what goes on in someone's head in those moments. I've been through it more than once since the beginning of winter.

That's how things have been done since the beginning of time at the Humberside rink.

But not tonight...

Nolan, the defeated captain, accuses Hooper of pulling before he was ready. Hooper, the winner of the tug-of-war, defends himself by saying he won according to the rules.

"Liar!" yells an angry Nolan.

What starts as a silly argument between two strutting roosters soon escalates. Blood boils, the captains jostle each other; it would only take a spark for a fight to break out.

Hooper and Nolan drop their sticks. Next will be the gloves...here we go! To make things worse, other players get involved. Hooper's friends take his side while Nolan's supporters rally behind him. This could easily turn into a riot; each side is convinced that the other side is wrong, and wants to knock some sense into it.

Me? Along with the few neutral boys who just want to play hockey, I wait for the outcome. I'm more amused than surprised to see that my brothers are in opposite camps. What's even funnier is that they're insulting each other, but with a smile, like they're playing a game. If a fight breaks out, Paul will throw himself at Muni, who is smaller than him, and they'll pretend to go at it. My older brother knows all too well that some hotheads his own age would take perverse pleasure in beating younger kids. And Muni is only eleven.

Between the screams and insults, I discover, to my great amazement, the real cause of this confrontation. Both captains want to pick first because of me! All of this for a girl who likes to play hockey with boys!

"Abby is on my team!" claims Hooper.

"She was on your team the last time. It's my turn to have her now," claims Nolan.

I've always been one of the last ones to be picked. Now suddenly, I'm in the category of the players most in demand. Hmmm.... Very nice.

A sharp whistle blast cuts through the air. It's Maurice Montgomery, the teenager in charge of the rink, and a giant who goes to Humberside Collegiate. Someone must have warned him about the explosive potential of the battle taking place on the ice.

"Did I hear you right, Hooper and Nolan? You're fighting over a girl?"

"Yes, but the girl is Abby Hoffman!" says Nolan.

And she's on my team!" indicates Hooper.

"No, on mine!" replies Nolan.

The two players go at each other again, rekindling the hostilities.

Another loud whistle blast.

"If you don't stop, I'll have to use the hose to cool you off!" warns Montgomery.

His threat dampens the captains' fire. He proposes a compromise. "Let Abby decide which team she wants to play with."

I watch the two teenagers, a few feet away from me. They're waiting for my choice, their eyes full of hope. I feel like making them wait. For once, they're in the vulnerable position of wanting to be picked, instead of being the ones deciding.

One of them will feel the embarrassment of not having been called first. A hard blow to his male pride.

The players around them grow impatient.

I don't leave them hanging any longer. "I choose... no one!"

Captain Nolan is overjoyed, but Hooper is furious. He's not used to having a player, and a girl at that, turn him down.

Realizing Nolan's mistake, I correct him. "No! I didn't say Nolan, I said no one!"

Now it's Hooper's turn to be thrilled while Nolan fumes.

"I just want to practice my slapshot so I can score my first goal before the end of the season."

Montgomery blows his whistle again and tells the two captains to make their teams. "And no fight!" he warns, with a mean face. "The hose is not very far away."

I skate off while Nolan and Hooper pick their players without much enthusiasm. In a corner behind the net, I throw down the puck that Jim Thompson gave me at the Gardens Saturday night. I hit it without stopping.

Chapter 24

More than 3,000 spectators have come to watch the first annual Little Toronto Hockey League Jamboree. The long evening during which nine games—yes, nine!—of thirty minutes each will be played, starts at 6:30 p.m. We take the ice at around nine o'clock.

The two teams—the St. Catharines Tee Pees and the Hamilton Cubs—are standing on their respective blue lines. Two special presentations are on the schedule. First, Ron Lowe, a Cubs player, is invited to center ice. His coach, Bob Bowden, gives him the "Little Hart Trophy," awarded to the most courageous and gentlemanly player in the league. Three years ago, Ron lost part of his right leg in a car accident. But this handicap never stopped him from playing hockey. The players from both teams bang their sticks on the ice as a way to salute his achievement.

Standing next to me, Scotty whispers in my ear, "Now get ready for a surprise, Hoffman."

"What surprise, Scotty? It was all over the papers!"

It's my turn to be called to center ice. As soon as my name is announced to the four corners of Varsity Arena, I receive a monster ovation that gives me shivers down my spine.

My captain, Jim Halliday, presents me with a trophy—a token of appreciation from the Tee Pees boys. The trophy is a hockey player in a classic pose, mounted on a wood base. On a plaque is the inscription: *To Abby Hoffman, from your fellow Tee Pees, Little Toronto Hockey League, 1956.*

"It's very nice," I say to Jim. "Thank you."

"You're welcome, Ab. It's our way of showing you that you're part of the team," he explains.

"The player on the trophy, is it a boy or a girl?" asks Ben Rose, the reporter from the *Star*.

"It's a girl dressed as a boy," answers Jim without missing a beat.

Several photographers are snapping shots of the presentation. One of them suggests we both hold the trophy. Our fingers touch by accident.

"Sorry," Jim apologizes.

It's too funny! I wear my brightest smile for the

photographers, proud to have been accepted, in the end, by this group of boys.

I skate to the bench and leave the trophy with the coach before going back to my position on our blue line.

The game is hard-fought. The Cubs and the Tee Pees are more or less equal. In the regular season rankings, we finished second behind the Toronto Marlboros, but four points ahead of the Cubs.

In the first period, I make a stupid mistake in my zone. Two players are battling for the puck in the corner near the net. I shout to David Kurtis that I'm on it. I rush toward the puck, determined to help my teammate. Bob Canning, the dangerous Cubs player, dekes and breaks free. I'm going after him…but the Tee Pees player comes right back and pushes Canning away from the puck. Carried by my momentum, I don't have time to brake. I crush a player from my own team against the boards. A solid bodycheck…

Poor Scotty. He won't have to tell his father, who is surely in the bleachers and can see for himself. He must think I did it on purpose and that I'm persecuting him.

The referee raises his arm and calls a penalty. "Number 6. Two minutes for obstruction."

"Serves you right, Hoffman," gloats Scotty, who can hardly stand upright.

Then follows a strange exchange between Captain Halliday and the referee.

"You can't punish, Ab!"

"Number 6 prevented the player from getting to the puck," the referee explains, his hands on his hips.

"Yes, but they're in the same team!"

"Doesn't matter," interjects Scotty, still unsteady on his legs. "It's the intention that counts."

After careful consideration, the referee admits to the mistake. He changes his decision and cancels my penalty. I thank Jim for stepping in.

"That was a solid bodycheck, Ab. You put all your heart in it," Jim says with a smile.

Scotty slowly goes back to the bench, grumbling, while his teammates make fun of him.

A third of the way through the game, our zone is again under threat by Bob Canning, the Cubs' best player, and the league's best scorer with eleven goals since the beginning of the season. He's a powerful shooter who terrorizes goalies. Before the game, Coach Grossi gave me a mission: as soon as Canning enters our zone, I have to be on him.

"Ab," he said during his speech in the locker room, "Canning is your man. I want you to follow him like a shadow, to stick to him like a second skin—you can't let him get away from you."

It took him a few seconds to realize what he'd just

said "your man" and "stick to him like a second skin." He started to blush. The players desperately tried to hold back their laughter.

"I...I get the idea, Mr. Grossi," I reassured him, a little uncomfortable.

So as Bob Canning dashes toward our goalie, ready to shoot, I knock him hard against the boards. Almost as hard as I did Scotty a few minutes earlier. Thrown out of balance by the impact, I fall with him. We both get up in a hurry. Our eyes meet.

If I had to guess all the potential reactions to my bodychecks, this one is the last one I would come up with. Canning takes off his right glove. That's it, he's ready to fight! But fights are not allowed in the Little Toronto Hockey League.

Canning's expression isn't aggressive. He extends his hand and shakes mine warmly. "It's an honor to have been bodychecked by you, Ab Hoffman!"

"Uh...thanks! I can do it again if you want," I tell him, stunned.

"Anytime!" he replies.

My first goal is still eluding me. So is Scotty's. He's out of luck in the beginning of third period. His back-hand hits the post to the left of the goalie. Scotty is so convinced that he has scored that he raises his arms in celebration.

The Cubs take advantage of Scotty's momentary

brain lapse to relaunch the attack. Bob Canning—him again—takes off on a spectacular breakaway the length of the ice, getting past four Tee Pees, including me. Luckily, David makes up for my slip. He stops him only feet from the net by stealing the puck.

The only goal of the game is scored not by Scotty or me, but by our very reliable Russell Turnbull during a clash in front of the Cubs' net. With less than two minutes to play, Russell pounced on a free puck and chipped it into the top of Hamilton's net.

Our goalie kept up his performance until the end, earning a shutout victory for the Tee Pees.

"This semi-final victory 1-0 against the Cubs was hard won thanks to everybody's efforts," says Mr. Grossi in the locker room after the game. "We're now going to the finals. Next Saturday, we play the winner of the Toronto-St. Michael's game."

I hurry to Earl Graham's office to get changed. With my skates around my neck and my trophy in my hand, I follow my father to a high section of the bleachers where we catch up with Mom. Little Benny is sleeping in her arms, exhausted. Paul and Muni are with their friends somewhere in the arena.

The ice has been cleaned and polished for the figure skating show by duo Barbara Wagner and Robert Paul.

Susie is in the first few rows near the boards. I can see she is hypnotized by her idols' performance. She was right—I know nothing about that sport other than the fact that the equipment and skates are different. What I do know, however, is that this performance—with pirouettes and dance and jumps—is breathtaking. The crowd gives them a generous round of applause when they exit.

"And now," announces the master of ceremonies who is dressed like a penguin, "the moment you've all been waiting for."

From center ice, he rotates a small glass drum filled with little pieces of paper. It's a bit insulting to suggest that people have come only for the draw of the "21-inch"—he stresses those words—black and white television. So we were only entertainment to distract the crowd from the wait? That's ridiculous. Yet the excitement in the arena is mounting. Next to me, a man sitting on the edge of his seat anxiously rubs his hands.

"We don't have a television," he explains to my mother.

"We don't either," replies Mom. "But we have a lot of books."

"Books? Hah!" says the man. "I'd rather watch hockey on television with my kids."

"Kids should play hockey outside, not watch it on TV," says Mom...rather uselessly.

The master of ceremonies pulls a piece of paper from the barrel.

"And the winner is...Mr. Holder from Simcoe."

Disappointed, our seat neighbor rushes out. Hundreds of spectators do the same, even though there are still two games in the program. It's terrible. The master of ceremonies was right: people came for the TV!

Five minutes later, two elderly people carefully make their way onto the ice to show their prize-winning ticket stub. I bet the newspapers will put a photo of them on the front page, and ignore all the games of the evening.

I should send a letter of apology to the *Toronto Daily Star* for doubting their judgment. I was completely wrong.

It's not a photo of the television winners that's on the front page of Saturday's newspaper. It's a picture of... me!

The large photo carries the headline "'The Boys' Honor Abby Hoffman For Hockey Skill.'" It was snapped just after I received the trophy from Jim Halliday. You can see both of us smiling and showing the trophy—without our fingers touching.

"Finally, good news on the front page!" exclaims Dad.

"Not a word about the television winners?" I ask, scanning the page.

"Not a word!" says Mom.

In a few sentences, the journalist explains why I was given the trophy. He also writes that although I didn't score my first goal, my defense work helped the Tee Pees to win.

"Yeah," I tell my parents. "Still no goal...But it's only a matter of time. Get your money ready!"

Chapter 25

When I glance at the calendar hanging on our kitchen wall, I realize how fast the days have gone by this winter: Wednesday, March 21st. The official arrival of spring, the fifteenth birthday of my big brother Paul...and almost the end of my season playing hockey in an organized league.

Winter in Toronto didn't linger for long this year. Already, the temperature has been happily above freezing on a few days. Skates are not in season anymore, at least not in the outdoor rinks, which have turned into puddles.

Winter jackets will be put away in the attic. But I'm not about to store this new one in a closet that reeks of mothballs. It came in the mail today. A package from

Montreal. A Montreal Canadiens jacket! It's a little big for me; I think it may fit Paul.

There's also a letter written on a typewriter. It's from Frank Selke.

"He's the Canadiens' coach," notes Dad. A fan of the Montreal Canadiens, my father is convinced they'll go home with the Stanley Cup this year.

"Dear Little Lady," Mr. Selke begins, *"I have heard of your participation in hockey and feel that such devotion to Canada's national game deserves a little reward.*

I brought up five little girls myself and appreciate all their good qualities, and I hope, in spite of the newspaper publicity you now receive, you will always remain as sweet as you are."

And it's signed by hand: *Frank Selke, G.M., Montreal Canadiens.*

There's also a P.S.: *"Maybe you've already scored your first goal? If that's the case, bravo! If not, I encourage you to keep working hard!"*

"If the Canadiens win the Stanley Cup, they might become my favorite team," I tell my father.

Paul and Muni are fighting over who will try on the jacket first. I'm holding it at arm's length and the sleeves almost fall to the floor. It could fit a grown man. I would float in it, for sure.

"I must look bigger in the paper," I say, trying to come up with an explanation.

"In a few years, it'll fit you like a glove," observes Mom.

"It's still a nice souvenir," adds Dad.

I'm a practical person, like my mother. I have no intention of hanging the Canadiens jacket in a dark closet, and waiting for the day when I'll slip my arms into the sleeves and see my hands at the other end.

I make a decision. Usually I inherit things worn by my brothers, this time it'll be the reverse: I'll give them something of mine. I offer the jacket to Paul.

"For your birthday, Paul! Happy Birthday! You get to wear it until Muni can put it on. Then Muni, you'll keep it until I'm big enough to fill it."

Paul immediately puts on the jacket and struts through the kitchen, proud as a peacock. Muni wants to try it on too. But for him, just like for me, the sleeves are way too long.

"It's very generous of you, Abby," remark my parents.

I shrug. "If it were a Red Wings jacket, it'd be different…"

Today, Thursday, March 22nd, the *Globe and Mail* reports that the Toronto Hockey League is opening its first hockey school for girls.

"Since the advent into boys' hockey of Abigail Hoffman,

there has been a demand for a Little Toronto Hockey League for girls.

Over 100 calls have prompted the league to take action and at 5:30 this evening at Varsity Arena, Little Nite Chairman Earl Graham will have a battery of instructors on hand to give the lassies their first lessons in the art of chasing pucks.

Admission to the school, which will last one hour per session, will be 25 cents."

Mr. Graham has invited me to the first session as a special guest. For free, he insisted. So I'm at Varsity Arena on this Thursday evening, surrounded by about forty girls aged six to fifteen. The article should have specified that girls had to wear hockey skates, not figure skates.

It's hard to skate and brake quickly with the teeth at the end of the figure skating blades. On top of that, the teeth gouge the ice.

The instructors—all men, what a surprise—direct the girls toward the locker room so they can put on their equipment. It's strange to not have to change in Chairman Graham's office. I look around; there are two dozen girls in the room. As a joke, I hit my jock twice.

POCK! POCK!

To my great surprise, five girls imitate me. We burst out laughing. They must have older brothers who play.

I hear a little girl cry in a corner of the room. Her mother is trying to comfort her while tying her skates. "I don't want to have short hair to play hockey," she sobs, her face lost in a heap of long blonde hair.

Someone must have told her that I had my hair cut short before I registered in the league. I reassure her and explain that short hair is not a requirement to play hockey.

Her mother thanks me. Julia, her daughter, is already smiling.

"But it's important to tie it up," I tell her. "Otherwise, if your long hair falls in your face, you won't be able to see the puck."

Julia pulls her hair back into a ponytail.

"There you go! Much better!"

I continue my observations. Over there, girls have skates too big for them or sticks taller than them by almost a foot. Close to me, Leslie Dabbage's father helps her put on her heavy goalie equipment. She whispers to him, "It's her, Abby Hoffman."

I'm wearing my Tee Pees jersey; the other girls are putting on jerseys from all four teams of the Little League. My bench neighbor, Mary Lynn Farrell, adjusts her Marlboros jersey. She even has an A, for Assistant Captain, embroidered next to the team's logo. "I play hockey at my school," she tells me. "Abby, do you think there'll be a girls' league next year?"

"Maybe. If not, cut your hair very short and don't tell anyone!"

This unique hockey school is generating a lot of interest outside of the rink. Journalists and photographers have come for the occasion and posted themselves near the players' bench. Impressed by Leslie Dabbage's elaborate goalie equipment, Phyllis Griffiths is trying to get a comment from her. A few nods is all she gets.

That's okay. Phyllis asks the photographer to take a shot of Leslie in front of her net. Leslie gets into position and stops moving. Entirely.

At the request of the man behind a TV camera, I skate toward Leslie, handling the puck. I opt for a weak shot to her left. She doesn't move a hair. The cameraman encourages Leslie to make a save. I start over; same shot but to her right this time, the side of her stick. Same result. Leslie doesn't react.

Take 3. This time, I know what to do. I throw the puck directly onto her pads. Like a tree cut through at its base, she slowly topples to the side.

"A real Gump Worsley!" I laugh.

She answers with a smile and remains lying on the ice, motionless. I skate up to her. "Get up, Leslie! Up!"

She tries to move but it proves impossible. Her equipment is too heavy for her. Lying on the ice, she reminds me of an upturned turtle!

Leslie finally gets help from the goalie instructor,

Denis Dejordy, who frees her from her unfortunate position.

Now that photographers and cameramen have finished, the hockey school takes off. The instructors insist on the importance of learning how to skate before learning how to play. The sticks are left in a corner and we do a few laps around the rink. Leslie, who still hasn't moved from her net, is escorted to the players' bench so she can rest.

A few girls have a hard time skating. But others are just as good as boys. Mary Lynn Farrell, in her Marlboros jersey, zooms across the ice. She's faster than me, that's for sure. She could definitely play in the current Little Toronto Hockey League. Anyone wanting to keep up with her would have to be in spectacular shape.

The weakest skaters are happy to finally retrieve their sticks, which they use not so much to hit the puck, but to prop themselves up. No surprise there because the phenomenon is not unique to girls. I remember seeing boys do the same thing after the registration session at Varsity Arena in November. In fact, in his first games, Scotty wasn't exactly a gazelle. And he's still not!

Exercises without the puck continue for about thirty minutes. But what everyone is hoping for, and anxiously waiting for, is the moment when the group will be divided in two. The dessert for the last ten minutes of the session: dark jerseys (Marlboros and Cubs) against light jerseys (Tee Pees and Majors). And what's great about this is that everyone is on the ice at the same time; about twenty girls on each side.

And we're all going after a single puck!

When the whistle announces the end of the hockey school session, the girls go back to the locker room. A few of them linger behind to shoot the puck in the net. A teenager lends a hand to little goalie Leslie, who made a few saves during the game without hurting herself.

Mary Lynn Farrell, who scored several goals during the session, walks down the hallway with me. "Good luck against the Marlboros on Saturday," she says. "I think several of us will be at the game to encourage you."

"That's nice. I'll do everything I can to score my first goal."

We enter the locker room. The atmosphere is electric, like after a huge victory. "You know, Abby," confides Mary Lynn, "what matters is not to score a goal. What matters is what you've accomplished this year on behalf of all the girls who like to play hockey. That's your goal!"

Leslie flies past us. Her goalie equipment is spread out on the floor. She's flapping her arms like a bird freed from its cage.

The next morning, just before leaving for school, I notice a new clipping on one of our bulletin boards.

"Hey! It's Leslie and Mary Lynn!" I say to my parents who are drinking coffee at the kitchen table. The girls are on the front page of the *Toronto Daily Star*, Friday, March 23rd.

The headline, however, is ridiculous: "Could It Be The Maple Leafs Will Sign One Of These?"

A brief caption—three lines—mentions that since the Abigail Hoffman episode, there's been a strong demand for a Little Toronto Hockey League for girls. The league has opened a hockey school for girls. Seven-year-old Leslie Dabbage shone in front of her net and ten-year-old Mary Lynn Farrell scored a few goals.

Another clipping, this time an article from the *Toronto Telegram*. The article has no byline, but my name appears in large type in the title: "Abby Still Waiting For Her First Goal."

It says that I have only two games left to put the puck in the opposing net: Friday night in the Little Toronto Hockey League All-Star Game, and the following day in the final against the Toronto Marlboros, who, the week before, won 3-0 in semi-final against the St. Michael's Majors.

Is it that important to score?

I think about what Mary Lynn Farrell said.

Yes! It's really important!

Chapter 26

"Abby, everyone knows that you're a girl now. Why don't you grow your hair long again?"

The question comes from someone my age: my friend, Susie Read. We're at Varsity Arena. Susie just left the ice after practicing for nearly an hour for her end-of-the-year show. Before getting reading for the all-star game, I can spend a few minutes with her.

"For the simple reason that it's more convenient when I swim. Short hair dries faster. You should try it."

"But long hair looks really good on you, Abby."

She doesn't convince me. "You know, Susie, when my hair gets to a certain length, it starts to curl and it makes my head look huge!"

Captain Jim Halliday, who has also been chosen for the all-star team, reminds me that we take the ice in twenty minutes.

Susie knows very little about my sport, and I know very little about hers. Offsides, the blue line, penalties— all of that is Greek to her. But she does read the papers. As I walk away, she shouts: "I hope you score your first goal tonight, Abby!"

I change in the office of the chairman, who's again driven out of the room by my presence. He doesn't complain, though I'm sure it must annoy him sometimes. But he can hardly say anything since he's the one who came up with this solution.

In the locker room the all-star players of the Little Toronto Hockey League have gathered. Our coach for the game is Mr. Bowden, who knew I was a girl from the beginning because his son is friends with my brother Muni. He greets me at the door.

"Welcome to the stars, Abby," he says in a friendly tone. "There's a place for you there, near Jim Halliday."

Mr. Bowden is a tall man with graying hair. His voice is gentle. When the Tee Pees play his Hamilton Cubs, I've noticed that he never yells at his players. He always encourages them. It must be nice to play for him.

When I walk into the room, all the players come to me to say hi.

"If you feel like crushing someone against the boards

like you did me, don't be shy," laughs Bob Canning of the Hamilton Cubs, the best scorer of all four teams.

I go to the place I've been assigned, next to Jim Halliday who slaps me on the shoulder. Russell Turnbull is at the other end of the room, next to defenseman David Kurtis. With four players, the Tee Pees are well represented.

We have one less player than the powerful Toronto Marlboros, easy to spot with their dark blue jerseys. Goalie Milt Dunnell Jr.—his father is a journalist for the *Toronto Daily Star*—sits next to my bench neighbor.

I don't feel like an intruder in this group. I have earned the right to be here. It's funny to think that if I hadn't been selected for this all-star game, no one would have discovered that Ab is actually an Abby.

During the warm-up, I take a moment to look up to the bleachers. There are a lot of people at Varsity Arena for a game that "has no importance" as the all-star coach, Mr. Bowden, put it. Good. That means more money for the Ontario Society for Crippled Children.

We're playing against all-star players from another section of the Little Hockey League. The two teams face each other, each on their blue line, for a series of special presentations before the game.

The first presentation is the most moving. It brings

tears to my eyes and puts me in mind of my parents' constant reminder: we're lucky to be healthy.

A boy my age, Chris Martin, rolls his wheelchair to center ice for the official faceoff. I'm sure he too would like to play hockey, or basketball, or swim or…simply walk.

Chris shakes the hands of the two captains. He drops the puck. A player picks it up and gives it to him as a souvenir. Then one of the organizers of this first Timmy Tyke Tournament hands him an $800 check for the Ontario Society for Crippled Children.

The boy leaves the rink to a standing ovation, pushed in his wheelchair by a woman I assume is his mother. Chris Martin rolls by me. His face is familiar…Hey! I recognize him! He's the boy who was at the hospital when I was there for my medical exam a few weeks ago. He's the one who smiled at me. How could I forget that?

"Have a good game, Abby Hoffman!" he wishes me.

I'm too choked up to thank him. No words come out of my mouth right now. I make a promise to myself. If I score my first goal tonight, I'll give him the puck.

At long last, the siren announces the beginning of the game.

Thirty minutes later, the end of the meet confirms that Mr. Bowden was right: this game had no importance.

The pace was slow and the players, not used to being on the same team, had trouble finding each other. Attacks were rare and there were too many offsides.

There were a few sparks when the teams set off the red light, but this all-star game won't go down in the history of local hockey. In the end, there was no winner. We tied. But there's still all the money raised for the kids. That's something!

Now I only have one more chance to score my first goal: tomorrow, during the final against the Toronto Marlboros. It will be the last game of my season.

Chapter 27

They're all here, in the bleachers of Varsity Arena, for this ultimate game between the Tee Pees and the Marlboros. With all the empty seats, familiar faces are easy to spot. The Tee Pees have played for hundreds of spectators before, but not this afternoon; with the exception of one section near our team's bench, the place is almost empty. Spring is in the air and people don't feel like spending their day inside an arena.

Still, they've all come. "They" are my parents and my three brothers (Paul, wearing the Canadiens jacket, his girlfriend, Erica Westbrook, on his arm); Phyllis Griffiths—for fun, not for work; my teacher, Ms. Morley; my school principal, Mr. Williams; my faithful friend

Susie; and the Junior Tee Pees assistant captain Ab McDonald (his friend Bobby Hull is officiating the game today). I also see several young girls from hockey school, including Leslie and Mary Lynn, and, near the boards, Chris Martin, the smiling young man in a wheelchair.

The Marlboros are the league's most powerful attackers; before I can think about scoring, I have to concentrate on my defensive work. The team's victory has priority over our individual performances, Coach Grossi emphasized before the game.

I don't get permission to put on my skates in the locker room, even though this is the last meet of the 1955-56 season.

On the ice, we gather around goalie Graham Powell. Jim Halliday reminds us about the coach's instructions. "No unnecessary risks. The Marlies are quick, it's up to us to slow them down."

We shout our team's rallying cry: Tee Peeeees!

As soon as Referee Hull drops the puck, the Marlboros, as expected, rush into our zone. A forward clears the puck in the corner. It's up to me to get it. I have my back to the action. I hear furious skating. An opponent charges me like a bull. I just have time to relay the puck to David Kurtis, who is positioned by the net, before I'm bodychecked against the boards. First thing I know, I'm kneeling on the ice, seeing stars.

Then, as if he just realized what he had done, the

Marlie player leans toward me. "I'm sorry, Abby. I didn't know it was you."

I come back to my senses, spring up, and push him roughly. "I don't want to be treated differently than the other players!"

It's so frustrating! I never asked to be treated differently! In our first games, the Marlboros didn't think twice about attacking me every chance they had. And now, just because they know I'm a girl, they want to spare me? It's an insult! I'm the same player with the same number 6.

The action continues in the opposite corner. David Kurtis is battling an opponent for the puck. I move toward the front of the net to protect my zone. The puck—*it's alive!*—comes back to my corner. The Marlboros player—the one who charged me—turns away to protect the puck and hit it to the blue line. Without hesitation, I body-check him. He crashes heavily on the ice. I steal the puck and clear my zone.

"And don't expect me to apologize!" I tell him.

I return to the bench, furious.

"Hey, Hoffman!" starts Scotty in his usual ironic tone.

"Shut up!" I shoot back in a tone that leaves no room for reply.

Still a little knocked out, the Marlies player slowly goes back to his bench. He throws a long stare at me.

"He got the message, Abby," says David. My anger

fades. I stop listening to Scotty.

"Of course! Mr. Kurtis has the right to speak!" Scotty sulks.

Word should get around on the Marlboros bench: no favors for Abby Hoffman. That's exactly what I want.

The brave Tee Pees don't cave under Toronto's repeated attacks. We fight to the death for every inch of the ice. The battle is fierce. Each team has an opportunity to score, but doesn't succeed. After first period, the game is tied 0-0.

Our goalie is brilliant. Twice he made a save on a breakaway. As for me, I didn't shoot at the Marlboros' net. I had my hands full with their forwards. And poor Scotty! Despite his efforts, he didn't score his much-coveted first goal. My mood slowly improving as the first period unfolds, I congratulate him for his work. "If you had been a puck, you would have finally scored!"

He told me off.

The thing is, while dashing toward the Marlboros net, Scotty tripped—and slid all the way into the net.

In hockey, like in any sport I imagine, some things are difficult to explain. For example, a team can dominate part of a game, and then suddenly the same team will be forced to the wall and have to fight for its life. We say that the wind suddenly turned.

That's what's happening in this game.

In the middle of second period, once again dominated by the Marlboros, our goalie makes a miraculous save. At the last second, he kicks his leg to the side, on a shot by center Bobby McGuinn that should have given the Marlies the lead.

Galvanized by Powell's feat, our team counters with a powerful wrist shot by Russell Turnbull in the top of their net—impossible to stop.

Two minutes later, while we're buzzing in the enemy zone, Jim Halliday receives a clever pass from David Kurtis and scores.

Losing 2-0, the Marlboros become nervous and make mistake after mistake. Undisciplined, not used to lagging behind like that, our opponents show their frustration. They engage in skirmishes with our players, swing their sticks viciously. One of their wingers takes advantage of the fact that Scotty skates with his head down to hipcheck him against the boards. The shock is so violent that Scotty loses both his glasses and his breath. He falls on the ice and squirms in pain.

I skate by to pick up his glasses so they don't get broken. But what's this round thing? It looks like…it's looking at me! It's…*it's an eye!*

Scotty catches his breath. He rubs his ribs. Suddenly, his hand flies up to his missing right eye.

The Marlboros player also discovers the eye on the

ice. He panics and swings his stick, ready to shoot this thing as far from him as possible.

"Nooo!"

Without thinking, I throw myself down to protect the eye. Carried by his momentum, the Marlboros player can't stop his stick. He hits my gloves.

I scream in pain. I'm sure he just crushed my fingers. My eyes well up with tears. The last time my hand hurt that badly was when Muni accidentally jammed my index finger and my thumb in a door.

Slowly, I open my gloves. The glass eye is not broken. David Kurtis hands Scotty his glasses. Half of his face still covered by his glove, Scotty searches the ice with his one good eye. He didn't see my rescue. Upset, he doesn't find anything. For one of the rare times in his life, he's speechless.

We're both taken to the locker room to recover. There's very little time left in second period anyway.

"Are you okay, Abby? Scotty?" asks Al Grossi.

I nod yes. Scotty stays silent. Mr. Grossi examines my bloody knuckles.

"I should be able to finish the game," I tell him.

Mr. Grossi turns to Scotty. He wants Scotty to remove the glove so he can assess the damage. "Were you hit by a stick? I couldn't see what happened from behind the bench," he says.

The "No!" that Scotty cries out is more an expression

of despair than pain. The Tee Pees coach doesn't insist and goes back to the game. "Come back as soon as you feel better, okay?" He closes the door behind him to give us some privacy. Scotty hides his face in his hands and bursts into tears.

"I'll never be able to play hockey again!" he sobs.

His distress touches me. He hasn't said a nice word to me since the beginning of the year, but he now looks completely helpless. I have the solution to his problem hidden in my glove.

Suddenly, I admire Scotty Hynek. In my mind, I go back through all the things that now make sense: his strange look sometimes, or his eyes not focused in the same direction, or the number of times he got body-checked because enemy players came at him from his blind spot.

But what I mostly remember is his panic during the eye test at the hospital. If it had been established that Scotty has only one eye, he would have been forbidden to play. This crazy boy played an entire season without anyone noticing his handicap!

I hit him in the flanks. "Here…"

He looks up. When he sees his glass eye in my hand, his face lights up.

"We all have our secrets, right, Scotty?" I say with a thin smile.

He gently picks up his prosthesis. What a shock! His

face is not covered anymore and there's an empty hole where the eye should be! He tells me he lost his eye when he was four years old. A branch pierced it. The injury was so severe, the doctors had to remove the eye. Without another word, he runs to the shower room.

In the meantime, Coach Grossi comes back to see how we're doing. "Where's Scotty?"

"He's taking a shower," I say as a joke.

Mr. Grossi turns white. "If Earl Graham discovers that you're in the same room as a boy taking a shower," he says in a trembling voice, "he's going to have a heart attack! And so will I!"

Right at this moment, Scotty comes back. Mr. Grossi is dumbfounded. "Weren't you in the shower?"

"Uh…no, I went to the bathroom."

"Third period is starting," the coach informs us. "Are you ready to go back? I need all my players."

Scotty glances at me. "You bet we are!" he says. Right, Hoffman?"

Mr. Grossi goes ahead, relieved to see us join the rest of the Tee Pees. In the hallway leading to the team's bench, Scotty grabs my jersey.

"Thank you uh…Abigail…for everything! If you hadn't picked up my eye…if—"

I interrupt him. "You would have done the same for me, right?"

Scotty hesitates for a second.

"Of course, not," I answer for him. "What was I thinking?"

"Let's go score this first goal!" Scotty replies.

Chapter 28

Back at the Tee Pees bench, Scotty and I don't have a chance to sit. The coach immediately sends us into the fray for the beginning of third period. I'm happy to see we're still leading 2-0, with ten minutes left to this final game.

Scotty goes to center line and takes his position at right wing for the faceoff, only to find himself next to the opponent who injured him in second period.

"Hey, Cyclops," the boy whispers.

Scotty is not at all shaken. "If you harass me or tell anyone about this, I'll take my eye out right in front of you, and I swear, what you'll see will give you nightmares for the rest of your life."

A trace of worry crosses the bully's face, and he skates off.

In nature, when wild animals are wounded, they become all the more dangerous. Their pride stung, the Marlboros do everything they can to turn the ship around.

During the first two minutes, they charge furiously at us. One of the shots hits the post. We're trapped in our zone. The mandatory shift change after two minutes gives us a breather, and fresh forces are sent on the ice.

Halfway through the period, during a massive charge from the Marlboros (following a penalty given to Scotty, who got back at the Toronto bully—an eye for an eye, as they say), our opponents score their first goal, a deflection shot. But the celebration is cut short by Referee Hull, who overturns the goal. He declares that the Marlies player intentionally changed the course of the puck with his skate to score the goal.

"We're not playing soccer, here!" he remarks to the coach, who asked for an explanation and ends up accepting the verdict.

This goal reversal knocks the wind out of the Marlboros who, right then and there, give up the fight. The blow is fatal. They don't have the energy to fight anymore; they simply defend themselves.

We have less than two minutes to play. In an ultimate attempt to shake his team out of its lethargy, the opposing coach removes his goalie.

I jump on the ice with David Kurtis, determined to help our goalie end the season with a shutout victory. But Coach Grossi has other plans for me. He puts Jim Halliday in my position and I take Jim's place to the left of center Russell Turnbull. Scotty Hynek is to his right.

"Time to score your first goal, Abby!" Jim reminds me.

Scotty looks at me from his side of the ice. He's shaking his head, exasperated. In spite of the recent events that brought us a little closer, the old Scotty quickly resurfaces.

"Everything for Hoffman, the Tee Pees' pet!" he grumbles, bitter. The fact that I'm being favored over him to score my first goal must seem terribly unfair.

The faceoff is in our zone. Screams rise from the bleachers: Abby! Abby! Abby!

The fan support for me is far from dampening Scotty's hostile attitude. For a second, I feel bad for him. But only for a second! Hey! I'm not about to apologize because my teammates and part of the crowd think highly of me!

According to a game plan drawn up by Coach Grossi, Scotty and I have to rush toward the Marlboro defensemen to neutralize them or intercept a pass.

That's exactly what happens. The Marlboros center wins the faceoff and relays the puck to his defenseman who shoots it toward our net. But the puck hits my pad and bounces forward beyond the red line. Since I'm in motion, I race alone toward the puck.

The ice is wide open in front of me. The two Marlboros defensemen, who didn't react fast enough, can't catch up. I cross into the Marlies zone. I see the empty net in front of me, about fifty feet away. The crowd gets louder. I hear a voice, very close, to my right.

"Here, Hoffman! Here!"

A voice that would normally make me grit my teeth. Except this time, the tone is so imploring that I don't have the heart to get angry.

Will I regret this one day? Maybe…but right now, it seems like the right thing to do.

I put the puck on the blade of Scotty's stick. (He finally understands the concept of keeping his stick on the ice…now that the season is over!)

Oh, no!

He's so surprised to receive the puck that he loses control of it. I already regret my decision. And there's a Marlboros player directly behind him.

What an idiot I am! In my desire to be generous with a teammate, I misjudged our chances. The way things are going, neither he nor I will score in this game.

Smart move, Abby…

I stop skating and glide toward the empty net. Here comes Scotty, the puck close to his skates. The enemy defenseman is about to steal it from him. Suddenly,

Scotty shows skills unseen until now. With his skate, he pushes the puck toward his stick and without so much as a look, shoots right in front of him.

The red light comes on!

"And scoooore!" screams Scotty, ecstatic, his arms raised to the sky.

He rushes to the net to retrieve the puck, escaping the congratulations of his own teammates.

●

Scotty spots his parents in the bleachers. He skates toward them, proudly holds up the puck, and throws it in their direction—with a little too much enthusiasm. The rubber disk hits a spectator exactly where his jock should be. The man lets out a high-pitched yelp while Scotty keeps cheering for himself.

Back at the center line for faceoff, Scotty goes silent to listen to the announcement of his goal: "The third goal of the St. Catharines Tee Pees was scored by number 8, Scotty Hynek!"

My turn to listen carefully: "With an assist from number 6, Abby Hoffman!"

Is it wishful thinking or do the cheers grow louder? Even Scotty notices. But nothing can ruin his good mood. Not even the "Abby! Abby!" resonating in the entire Varsity Arena.

As soon as the announcer broadcasts the time of

the goal—8 minutes 48 seconds—Scotty starts screaming again. The referee, who is ready for the faceoff, has
to blow his whistle twice to get him to shut up. He even
threatens to send him to the penalty bench for delaying
the game!

Despite Jim Halliday's protestations, I go back to my
defense position.

"There's a little over a minute left," he insists.

True. Except the Marlboros goalie is back in front
of their net. The coach must have decided that a 3-0 loss
would be more honorable than a 4-0 or 5-0 loss.

I prefer to end my season in the same position I have
played since the fall.

The game starts up again, but without much intensity. Scotty keeps floating on a cloud. He doesn't skate
toward the puck. He walks and dances on the spot with
a blissful—or stupid, depending on who you're asking—
smile on his face. Seeing him like this makes me glad
about my decision. I'm really happy for him.

In any case, my job is to stop the enemy forwards,
not to put the puck in our opponent's net.

Chapter 29

After the siren seals the outcome of the game, the Tee Pees rush toward Graham Powell. Panicked at the sight of this mob descending on him, Powell seeks refuge behind his net. We manage to calm down a bit, and a little reassured, Graham lets us approach him. He's immediately surrounded by fourteen team members who hit his pads with their sticks, and cheer him with slaps on the back, shoulders and stomach. Coach Grossi joins in the celebration. We all shout our rallying cry: Tee Peeeees!

Scotty, still excited about his goal, keeps on hitting the players' pads. He doesn't look where his stick is landing so Mr. Grossi becomes his victim. Now the coach is jumping up and down on one leg, holding the other leg with both hands.

"That's a funny victory dance, Mr. Grossi," says Scotty.

During this celebration, every Tee Pees member is carried on a group of players' shoulders while his name his chanted out loud. Captain Halliday is the first to get the honor. Then it's the turn of goalie Powell, who is much heavier with all his equipment.

The Marlboros players—with heads slung low and heavy hearts—wait at their blue line to shake our hands. It must be humiliating for them to watch the Tee Pees' celebrations, especially since they dominated the league during the regular season.

Jim Halliday puts an end to the laps of honor right before Scotty's turn. He invites us to go shake hands with our defeated rivals. Scotty stands next to me in the Tee Pees line.

"I bet they'll all remember your name."

A minute later, Scotty is proved right. To have an opponent call you by name is very nice. It feels like a sign of respect. Unfortunately for them, I only remember the names of their best scorer, Bobby McGuinn, and their goalie, Milt Dunnell Jr.

We go back to the locker room, our fans still cheering. I rush to Earl Graham's office so I can take off my skates and join my teammates.

Passing the Tee Pees locker room, I see the chairman unlocking his door. "One last time?" I say, in a hurry.

"No," says, pointing to the room where the Tee Pees are going. "Your things are in there."

Did I thank him? I think I did. I hurry to my team's locker room, afraid he'll change his mind. My boots and my coat are at my place between David Kurtis and Scotty Hynek. I'm greeted with cheers of "Abby! Abby!"

I sit down to take off my skates. David Kurtis gives me a big hug. "It was very nice playing with you, Abby Hoffman. Should we do it again?"

"Uh…"

In truth, I haven't thought about next year. I just want to enjoy the present moment, even if it is in Scotty's company.

"Did you see my goal? Did you see my goal?" he shouts, totally wired, trying to get his teammates to admire him or at least pay attention to him. "Hoffman's pass was terrible, but I managed to catch it and to score. Did you see my goal?"

Good old Scotty. He'll never change.

"The puck was right on your blade," David remarks.

"Yes, the blade of my skate! Did you see my foot-work to retrieve Hoffman's awful pass?" continues Scotty, as if he hadn't heard a word.

"Yes, Scotty," I say. "Very clever!"

He's not listening. Just yesterday he would have

gotten on my nerves, but today he makes me laugh.

Excitement in the locker room goes up a notch when the parents arrive. Mine make their way to me. They hug me, proud of my accomplishments.

"It was very generous of you to let your teammate with the glasses score," says Dad.

"I'm giving you the rate for a goal, not an assist," promises Mom, as she searches her purse for a dollar.

Paul, Muni and Little Benny join us. I grab my older brothers by their coat sleeves and whisper in their ears: "It's true that you're my idols!"

Confused, Paul looks at my parents. "I think Abby took a puck to the head."

Oh, here's my friend Susie!

"Hey, Abby. Where are the showers?" she whispers with a chuckle.

With players as young as us, there won't be beer or champagne to celebrate this championship like there was for the Detroit Red Wings after they won the Stanley Cup. Orange Crush is brought in for us. Each player gets his own uncapped bottle.

"Orange Crush?" says Scotty, still wired. "Hey! We're celebrating! Give me something stronger! I want a Coke!"

"You're hyper enough as it is, Scotty," remarks his mother.

Al Grossi claps his hands and asks for silence in the room. He raises his bottle: "Gentlemen"—he hesitates for a second—"and young lady," he adds, which generates a few laughs. "I drink to your success, your hard work, and your team spirit. I'm thrilled to have been your coach this year."

His voice cracks with emotion. We raise our bottles high and clink them together almost to the point of breaking.

"To my first goal!" exclaims Scotty who does a round so every teammate can drink to his achievement. When he gets to me, he pauses for a few seconds. I try to remember on which side his glass eye is. Right or left? Even from this close, I can't tell.

He turns to the Tee Pees. "Hey, guys! Let's raise our bottles in honor of Abby Hoffman's season!"

I'm stunned.

"A fabulous season, Abby Hoffman! Thank you!" shouts Scotty.

Once again, the players' voices fill the room, led by Jim Halliday: "Abby! Abby! Abby!"

Happy and touched, I shout the team's rallying cry, which is immediately echoed by my teammates. "Tee Peeeees!"

BY WAY OF OVERTIME

From March 25, 1956 to today

The hockey career of young Abby Hoffman, born in Toronto on February 11, 1947, ended quite simply in the early spring of 1956. Abigail abandoned the sport, or at least its organized form—she continued to play at the Humberside rink—to concentrate on basketball, swimming, and, most of all, on running.

The Little Toronto Hockey League did not create a hockey league for girls the following fall. In a December 1956 interview with a CBC radio journalist, Abby explained that the officials of the league abandoned the idea because it would have been too expensive to rent the ice for girls.

We can assume that this was the main reason Abby abandoned hockey. According to a comment by the same journalist, she might have been refused access to the boys' league. Not only did the officials of the Little Toronto Hockey League fail to change their minds the following year, but also, in November 1958, they went so far as to adopt an amendment preventing the creation of a mixed league. This was directly related to the Abby Hoffman episode from two years earlier. In the league's constitution, any future Abigail was eliminated by the words "for boys."

The determination that carried Abby through that hockey season never left her. Over the years, Abby Hoffman built an international career for herself as a runner. However, resistance to girls' hockey is not the only obstacle that Abby had to overcome in her life. In high school, she realized that boys were encouraged to be physically active, while few similar opportunities were offered to girls. At a track and field meet in Waterloo, Ontario in the summer of 1961, she was supposed to run a 220-yard race in the "girls-under-fifteen" category. The event was cancelled because the organizers decided the distance was too great for girls. Abby registered for the half-mile race.

In addition, at the time, women were not allowed to participate in events over 800 yards. Once again, Abby had to spend time and energy to have this ban lifted. In

1966, she fought to get the University of Toronto's Hart House—home to the only indoor running track—to open its doors to women after having been expelled from the track three times.

This initiative was commemorated at Hart House in 1979 with a plaque bearing the inscription: "Only she who attempts the absurd will achieve the impossible."

Abby became one of the best middle-distance runners in Canada. At fifteen, though she had been running for only a year, she represented her country at the 1962 Commonwealth Games in Perth, Australia.

Four years later, the Canadian Champion won gold medal in the 880-yard event at the Jamaica Commonwealth Games, while pursuing her studies in Political and Economic Sciences at the University of Toronto.

The woman who, as a young girl, dreamed of going to the Olympics, participated in four Games: Tokyo (1964), Mexico City (1968), Munich (1972) and Montreal (1976), where she was Canada's flag-bearer in the opening ceremony. The members of the Canadian team selected her in recognition of her long international career, and to thank her for her work with the Canadian Olympic Association.

It's also worth noting that in the mid-70s, this articulate and independent woman was one of the people who dared speak out about Canadian elite athletes' poor financial conditions. A bursary program was set up to remedy the situation, allowing athletes to concentrate on their training, without having to worry too much about financial issues.

Abby's greatest moment in all her years of track and field, she told author Fred McFadden in her book *Abby Hoffman*, was her performance in the 880-yard (800 meters) finals at the Munich Games. Competing against seasoned runners, she managed to beat the Olympic record of the time.

Abigail Hoffman retired from the track at the end of the 1970s, after an international career that saw her on the podium multiple times. She spent many years working at Sports Canada in Ottawa (she was the first female Director General) before moving to Health Canada. In 1993, she became the first Director General of the Bureau of Women's Health And Gender Analysis.

Her career earned her much public recognition. On October 20, 1982, she was named Officer of the Order of Canada. The following year, the Abby Hoffman Cup was inaugurated by the Ontario Women's Hockey Association to reward the best team in Canada's first National Women's Hockey Championship. In November 1994, the University of Toronto inducted her into its Hall of Fame. Ten years later, she was admitted into Canada's Sports Hall of Fame.

The Canadian Association for the Advancement of

Women and Sport and Physical Activity awarded her the Herstorical Award in February 1992, to recognize her efforts in advocating for gender equality in sports. Five years earlier, at the gala for the same association, Abby Hoffman gave the Breakthrough Award to 15-year-old hockey player Justine Blainey. This young Ontarian had to go all the way to the Commission on Human Rights to be able to play hockey in a boys' league. It took her three years to win her case.

Since 1995, Ms. Hoffman has represented Canada as council member of the International Association of Athletics Federations. In 2007, the International Olympic Committee awarded her the Women In Sports Award for the Americas.

At the time of publication of this book, Abby Hoffman was Assistant Deputy Minister for the Strategic Policy Branch at Health Canada.

Dorothy Medhurst

Abby Hoffman's mother, Dorothy Medhurst, passed away while the author was working on the first draft of this novel. She died on December 29, 2010, at the age of 95. She was living with her son Benny in the family house on Glendonwynne Road in Toronto.

Until late in life, she lived in a cabin in Caledon with no phone, electricity or running water.

This passionate woman was an artist. As a teenager,

she taught art to children at Toronto's Art Gallery of Ontario, under the direction of painter Arthur Lismer, a member of the famous Group of Seven. The more time she spent with children, the more drawn she was to the excitement and rewards of teaching. She continued to instil the love of art in youth well into her eighties.

Sault College in Sault Ste. Marie, Ontario, annually gives out the Dorothy Medhurst Award to a second-year student in Early Childhood Education who demonstrates creativity through an innovative and energetic approach. Her curiosity never faded over the years.

Dorothy Medhurst is also the subject of the film *Notes On Seeing*.

Samuel H. Hoffman

Abby's dad was right when he predicted the end of the Detroit Red Wings' supremacy in the National Hockey League. Spring 1956 saw the beginning of the Montreal Canadiens' domination over the next five years.

Samuel Hoffman predeceased his wife. He was a fervent supporter of track and field, and was one of the directors of the Toronto Olympic Club. He died on July 21, 1978 at the age of 69. A retired chemist, he was struck by a heart attack while volunteering as an equipment attendant for the Junior Track & Field Championship at the Etobicoke Centennial Stadium.

Paul Hoffman

Abby's brother Paul is one of the most fascinating characters in this gallery of people who were important in Abby's life. Born on March 21, 1941, Paul became an internationally renowned geologist, as a result of his studies and work on the Snowball Earth theory. According to his research, 600 or 700 million years ago, the Earth would have been covered in ice over long periods, with every glacial period lasting as long as several million years. Frequent stays in Namibia (Africa), where he studied layers of sedimentary rock, brought him to this conclusion.

Dr. Paul Hoffman worked in the Department of Earth and Planetary Sciences at the prestigious Harvard University in Cambridge, USA. He is now affiliated with the University of Victoria in British Columbia. He received the 2009 Wollaston Medal—the highest award granted by the Geological Society of London. Graciously, Paul Hoffman answered several of my questions via email.

Muni Hoffman

Muni was considered the most talented hockey player in the Hoffman family. When he boasted about his 38 goals in regular season play, he wasn't exaggerating. Muni joined the Ontario Junior Hockey League as a defenseman. In 1961, he played for the Toronto Marlboros. The following year, he wore the colors of the Whitby Dunlops in the Metro Junior A League. A year later, he went back to the Ontario Junior League, this time playing for the Oshawa Generals. The experience didn't pay off and he was drafted by the Lakeshore team in the Junior B League.

Muni Hoffman ended his junior career as captain of the Weston Dodgers in 1964-65. With six new franchises accepted in the National Hockey League in the 1967 season, Muni was invited to the Los Angeles Kings training camp. Unfortunately, his services were not retained.

Phyllis Griffiths

Journalist Phyllis Griffiths was born in Britain in 1905. She had a remarkable basketball career throughout the 1920s and '30s as an athlete, coach and referee. The daily *Toronto Telegram* newspaper hired her in 1927. She was one of the first women columnists in Canada to write about sports. Her column, titled *The Girl and The Game*, was published for about fifteen years. When she met Abby Hoffman in March 1956, she was 51 years old.

Respected in her profession, Ms. Griffiths was inducted into the Canadian Newspaper Hall of Fame on March 22, 1978.

She died in December 1978.

Foster Hewitt

Foster Hewitt (1902-1985) also had an interesting career. He was the voice of hockey in English Canada, both on radio and television, from one ocean to the other.

For forty years, he did play-by-play commentary for *Hockey Night in Canada*, the first widely listened-to radio show in Canada. After the arrival of television in the 1950s, he was broadcast simultaneously on CBC radio and TV until 1963. He is known for his famous: "He shoots! He scores!" He met Abby Hoffman in the gondola at Maple Leaf Gardens in Toronto. This same gondola was dismantled in August 1979 and replaced with executive suites. The current media gondola at the Air Canada Center in Toronto was named after him.

Foster Hewitt was inducted as Builder into the Hockey Hall of Fame in 1965, and named Officer of the Order of Canada in 1972. A trophy—the Foster Hewitt Memorial Award, presented by the Hockey Hall of Fame—is given every year to members of the radio and television industry who make outstanding contributions to their profession.

The Junior Tee Pees

A few players from the Junior St. Catharines Tee Pees made their mark in the National Hockey League. By the way, the Toronto Marlboros, who lost in semi-finals against the Tee Pees, won the Memorial Cup that year (1956) against the Regina Pats.

The most spectacular Junior Tee Pees player was no doubt Bobby Hull, who did officiate a few games in the Little Toronto Hockey League during his time with the Tee Pees.

Born in 1939, Bobby Hull was one of the greatest National Hockey League players of his time. Hired at eighteen by the Chicago Black Hawks (season 1957-58), he played with that team until 1971-72. Nicknamed the Golden Jet, Hull helped the Black Hawks win the Stanley Cup in 1960-61—their first Cup in twenty-three years. With teammate Stan Mikita, he developed the curved hockey stick. Traveling over 160 km per hour, his slapshot used to terrorize goalies. He was named Best Player of the NHL in 1965 and 1966. After the creation of the World Hockey Association, he went to Winnipeg where he wore the Jets colors starting in 1972, then joined the Hartford Whalers. He retired in 1980 after accumulating an astounding 610 goals and 1170 points. He was inducted into the Hockey Hall of Fame in 1983.

Ab McDonald, assistant captain of the St. Catharines Tee Pees, went from the Ontario Junior League to the Rochester Americans in the American Hockey League in 1956. He signed with the Montreal Canadiens in 1957. With the Canadiens, this left winger won three consecutive Stanley Cups. He was then traded to the Chicago

Black Hawks where he reunited with his friend Bobby Hull and won a forth Stanley Cup! In the following years, McDonald played with different teams (Boston, Detroit, Pittsburgh and St. Louis) before ending his career with the Winnipeg Jets, once again alongside his friend Bobby Hull. In 762 games in the National Hockey League, Ab McDonald scored 182 goals and a total of 430 points.

Elmer Moose Vasko is another member of the Tee Pees who contributed to the Chicago Hawks' conquest of the Stanley Cup in 1960-1961. This giant defenseman (6 feet 2 inches), originally from Duparquet in the province of Quebec, played for Chicago until 1965 after leaving St. Catharines in 1956. He finished his career with the Minnesota North Stars. Moose Vasko amassed 200 points in thirteen regular seasons. He died in October 1998.

The Maple Leafs

Three players from the Toronto Maple Leafs who met Abby Hoffman, had great careers in the National Hockey League.

Right winger Tod Sloan played with the Leafs for almost ten years (1948-1957) before being traded to the Chicago Black Hawks in 1959. The following year, he helped Chicago win the Stanley Cup with teammates Bobby Hull and Ab McDonald. Tod Sloan retired in 1962. In 745 games with the NHL, he scored 220 goals.

Right defenseman Jim Thompson wore only one jersey in his twelve seasons with the NHL: the Toronto Maple Leafs'. He scored 234 points in 787 games.

Finally, the other Jim—Morrison this time—played for the Leafs from 1951 to 1958. The defenseman then left Toronto to go to Boston, Detroit, and New York. He was with the Quebec Aces in the American League from 1960 to 1967, before a brief return to the NHL with the Pittsburgh Penguins. In 704 games, he accumulated 200 points.

It is impossible not to mention the Toronto Leafs player George Armstrong—nicknamed the Chief. This player (whom Susie refers to when she's talking to Abby) wore the Leafs jersey for 21 seasons (1951 to 1971) and played 1188 games. He became team captain in 1957. He was inducted into the Hockey Hall of Fame in 1975, after scoring 296 goals and 713 points.

Stars on skates

Abby Hoffman's best friend Susie Read was right to praise the figure skating performances of Barbara Ann Scott and the Wagner-Paul pair.

Originally from Ottawa, Barbara Ann Scott (born in 1928) earned her place in the Canadian collective memory by winning a gold medal in the St. Moritz Olympics in Switzerland on February 6, 1948. Barbara Ann Scott was named Canadian Athlete of the Year in 1945, 1947, and 1948. She then participated in ice revues until 1954. She had to wait almost four decades before being named Officer of the Order of Canada in 1991, and was inducted into the Sports Hall of Fame in 1995. She died in September of 2012.

Barbara Wagner and Robert Paul dominated the world scene in pairs figure skating for the second half of the 1950s. In addition to being Canadian Champions five times, they were World Champions from 1957 to 1960, and won a gold medal in the 1960 Winter Olympics in Squaw Valley, CA, becoming the first Canadian athletes in this discipline to climb to the top of the podium. Wagner and Paul retired from the amateur circuit in 1960 to skate with the professionals until 1964. The Skate Canada Hall of Fame opened its doors to them in 1993.

The arenas

The hockey games in this story take place, for the most part, at two Toronto arenas: Varsity and Maple Leaf Gardens.

Opened on December 17, 1926, Varsity Arena was one of the first arenas built without the steel pillars that used to obstruct the spectators' view. It seats more than 4,000 people. The building is located at 275 Bloor Street West near the University of Toronto.

Maple Leaf Gardens was built in 1931 and was home to the Maple Leafs until 1999. The NHL team played its last game there on February 12 before moving to the Air Canada Center, thus putting an end to a 67-year tradition. This hockey temple, still located at the corner of Church and Carlton Streets in Toronto, is the last of the six original arenas in the history of the league. It has been repurposed and now serves as an athletic center for Ryerson University.

Bibliography

Digital archives

"Ab turns out to be a girl." CBC Digital Archives (radio), broadcast 20 December 1956.

"A rising star: Abby Hoffman at 15." CBC Digital Archives (radio), broadcast 23 February 1962.

"He's a girl." CBC Digital Archives (television), broadcast 9 March 1956.

Books

Miner, Valerie. "A portrait of Abby Hoffman." *Her Own Woman: Profiles on Ten Canadian Woman.* Macmillan of Canada, 1975.

McFadden, Fred. *Abby Hoffman, Super People Series.* Fitzhenry and Whiteside, 1978.

Hall, M. Ann. *The Girl and the Game.* Broadview Press, 2002.

Newspaper articles

"Little THL Resumes Nov. 19 At Varsity." *Toronto Daily Star*, 12 November 1955.

Proudfoot, Jim. "Playing, Not Winning That Counts." *Toronto Daily Star*, 23 December 1955.

MacDonald, John. "Ref Hands Out Tips As Well As Penalties in Little THL." *Toronto Daily Star*, 7 February 1956.

Rose, Ben. "No time for Girls—Abby." *Toronto Daily Star*, 9 March 1956.

"Abby Concedes Leafs Slightly Better Than Own Team." *Toronto Daily Star*, 12 March 1956.

"Ab Hoffman Gets Award at Little THL Jamboree." *Toronto Daily Star*, 15 March 1956.

"They're Both Tee Pees." *Toronto Daily Star*, 16 March 1956.

"The Boys' Honor Abby Hoffman For Hockey Skill." *Toronto Daily Star*, 17 March 1956.

Young, Jerry. "Goalies Dominate Little THL Scene." *Toronto Daily Star*, 17 March 1956.

"THL Hockey School For Girl Tonight." *Toronto Daily Star*, 22 March 1956.

"Could It Be The Maple Leafs Will Sign One Of These?" *Toronto Daily Star*, 23 March 1956.

"Abby Seeks Her First Goal In Timmy Tyke Tournament." *Toronto Daily Star*, 29 March 1956.

Griffiths, Phyllis. "Rough, Hardchecking Ab Back On The Ice—She Is." *The Toronto Telegram*, 8 March 1956.

Griffiths, Phyllis. "A Girl Hockey League." *The Toronto Telegram*, 9 March 1956.

"She's A Star." *The Toronto Telegram*, 9 March 1956.

Hoffman, Abby. "Tod's Stick, Leaf Cushions Wonderful, New To Abby." *The Toronto Telegram*, 11 March 1956.

Griffiths, Phyllis. "Abby Was Star, Fan, Mascot." *The Toronto Telegram*, 12 March 1956.

Morganson. "Abigail Still A Winner—Her Teeps Champions." *The Toronto Telegram*, 17 March 1956.

"'Stay As Sweet As You Are'—Selke Sends Ab A Sweater." *The Toronto Telegram*, 2 April 1956.

"Name Nine-Year Old Girl To Boys' All-Star Team." *The Globe and Mail*, 9 March 1956.

"To Give Girls Hockey Lessons." *The Globe and Mail*, 22 March 1956.

Rosenfeld, Bobbie. "Mustangs Royally Treated, Coach Vince Leah Reveals." *The Globe and Mail*, 4 April 1956.

"Great Pretender: Girl, 9, Hockey Ace." *The New York Times*, 8 March 1956.

"Les officiels d'une petite ligue de hockey confondus." Library and Archives Canada (www.collectionscanada.gc.ca), *La Presse*, 9 March 1956.

About the Author

Alain M. Bergeron is a big hockey fan. He is a prolific author of books for young people. He lives in Victoriaville, Quebec.